He'd resigned himself to doing his duty toward her and their child—nothing else. Just his duty.

But now, someone had hurt her and could have hurt his baby. Something primal swelled up within him, adding to the mix of anger and that other emotion he couldn't name.

"Rache," he said, "I swear, I'm going to find out who did this. And until I do, I'm not letting you out of my sight. You and that baby are my responsibility, and I'll be damned if I let anyone get close enough to hurt you again."

Rachel's brow wrinkled and she looked down at the water glass.

She hadn't liked what she'd heard, and he knew why. His intention had been to reassure her, but it hadn't come out exactly right. He'd sounded harsh and angry.

It appeared she didn't believe him. She had to know he could take care of her. So why did he get the feeling she didn't want him to?

MALLORY KANE

DETECTIVE DADDY

Harlequin®

TORONTO NEW YORK LONDON
AMSTERDAM PARIS SYDNEY HAMBURG
STOCKHOLM ATHENS TOKYO MILAN MADRID
PRAGUE WARSAW BUDAPEST AUCKLAND

For the girls at the beach house.

Special thanks and acknowledgment to Mallory Kane for her contribution to the Situation: Christmas series.

Recycling programs
for this product may
not exist in your area.

ISBN-13: 978-0-373-69567-6

DETECTIVE DADDY

ABOUT THE AUTHOR

Mallory has two very good reasons for loving reading and writing. Her mother was a librarian, who taught her to love and respect books as a precious resource. Her father could hold listeners spellbound for hours with his stories. He was always her biggest fan.

Mallory loves romantic suspense with dangerous heroes and dauntless heroines, and enjoys tossing in a bit of her medical knowledge for an extra dose of intrigue. Mallory lives in Mississippi with her computer-genius husband and three exceptionally intelligent cats.

She enjoys hearing from readers. You can write her at mallory@mallorykane.com or via Harlequin Books.

Books by Mallory Kane

*Ultimate Agents
**Black Hills Brotherhood
‡‡The Delancey Dynasty

CAST OF CHARACTERS

Ash Kendall—A decorated police detective, Ash is deeply dedicated to finding justice for victims. Off duty, though, he's a Casanova. After his parents were killed on Christmas Eve in a brutal double murder, Ash set out to enjoy life to the fullest. But his carefree life is about to come to a screeching halt when his ex reveals she's pregnant with his child.

Rachel Stevens—The DNA specialist has not one but two pieces of devastating news for her ex-boyfriend Ash Kendall. The man convicted of killing his parents is innocent. And if that's not enough, Rachel is pregnant.

Deputy Police Chief Charles Hammond—He headed the original investigation into the Kendall murder. Catching the killer catapulted him to the top of his field. But is his obsession with proving that he arrested the right man twenty years ago clouding his judgment?

Rick Campbell—Twenty years ago, this small-time thief was arrested in the Kendalls' neighborhood with stolen items in his possession. Now he's been exonerated of their murder and set free. Is he really innocent?

Tim Meeks—This ambitious assistant district attorney knew if he could convince the police commissioner to retest Campbell's DNA, it was a win-win situation for him. Would he go so far as to contaminate the DNA to further his career?

Craig Kendall—He raised his brother's children as his own after Joseph Kendall and his wife were murdered. Now new DNA findings have proven that Rick Campbell is innocent. The news sends Craig over the edge. Is he capable of taking the law into his own hands and going after Campbell, no matter what the evidence says?

Chapter One

Ashton John Kendall stormed through the squad room, ignoring the curious gazes of his fellow detectives. He headed straight toward the back, where the Crime Scene Investigations unit had their desks.

He hadn't slept a wink the night before, after delivering the bad news to his family. God, that had been hard.

He could have talked to Rachel last night as well, but— no. He'd been too angry. Way too angry.

Problem was, eight hours of tossing and turning hadn't lessened his fury one bit. Hell, he hadn't even stopped at the coffee shop for his usual coffee and casual flirting with the blonde barista.

He rounded the corner and skidded to a halt. That was odd. Rachel wasn't at her desk.

She was *always* here by this time. He glanced at his watch to be sure. Eight-thirty. During the weeks when they'd dated, he'd found out how obsessive she was about being on time. She liked to get any paperwork out of the way first thing before heading to the lab, so her schedule would be clear in the case of an emergency.

"Damn it, where is she?" he snapped to no one in particular.

"Good morning, Ash," the transcriptionist sitting at a tiny computer table against the wall said.

He smiled at her and tried to tamp down his anger. "Hi, Vanessa. How's your brother?" He and Vanessa had dated for a short while a couple of years ago. They'd had fun.

She beamed at his question. "He's doing really well. He's acting like his old self again."

"I'm glad. A shame that he had to go through a triple bypass at thirty-three. Have you seen Rachel?"

Vanessa shook her head. "No. She's been late a couple of days this past week. She should be in anytime now."

Rachel Stevens late for work—and not once but several times?

Jack Bearden walked in with a steaming cup of coffee. "Morning," he said. He, Rachel and Frank Marino were the senior criminalists for the Ninth District of the St. Louis Metropolitan Police Department.

"What about the lab? Could she be down there?" Ash asked Vanessa.

"Maybe, but I doubt it. You know how she likes to clear her desk first thing in the morning."

Ash took a deep breath, working to control the anger that was building up again. "Tell Rachel I need to talk to her as soon as she—"

"Ash?"

He whirled around to see Rachel standing there, clutching a big leather purse. She looked pale. "Here I am," she said, spreading her hands and offering a smile that looked pasted on.

Just seeing her ramped up his anger another notch. "Yeah, we need to talk," he snapped.

Rachel ducked her head and slid past him to her desk. She laid down her purse and started to take off her raincoat, but apparently decided to leave it on. She slid her fingers around the back of her neck to free her ponytail.

"Have a seat," she offered, pointing to a straight-back chair.

"Not—here," he grated.

Rachel looked up, startled, as did Vanessa and Jack. Ash sucked in a breath and consciously relaxed his jaw. "Can we—?" He inclined his head in the general direction of the squad room.

She studied his face, her own still pale, her lips pressed tightly together. Then she nodded and stepped past him.

"Where?" she asked evenly.

"Room three." Interrogation Room Three wouldn't be occupied unless there had been a drug raid or a gang war during the night. Sure enough it was empty.

Ash held the door for her, then closed it behind him. Rachel sat down and folded her arms. She looked miserable—and guilty. As well she should.

But she also looked small and scared. A hollow feeling in the middle of his chest, which had been there ever since he'd cooled things between them, began to throb. He rubbed the spot with his knuckles. Maybe it was indigestion.

"Ash?" Rachel said tentatively. "Will this take long? Because I've got a lot to do this morning."

He quelled the urge to stand over her as if she were a suspect. Instead he pulled out a chair across from her and sat, flattening his palms on the tabletop.

Rachel watched him, her eyes wide in her pale face. Pink spots rose in her cheeks. Her throat moved as she swallowed.

She looked frightened. He knew he could be formidable. His brothers used to call him *the berserker* when they were kids. But he'd never turned his wrath on a woman. With an effort, he composed his face. He wanted her to speak first. Wanted her to own up to what she'd done without him having to drag it out of her. Own up and apologize.

She frowned and her gaze dropped to his hands. She took a long, shaky breath. "Ash, I don't know what you've heard—"

"You don't?" he interrupted, irritated by her hedging. "Really? You didn't think I'd find out eventually? I guess you hoped I wouldn't get wind of it until the official announcement."

Rachel recoiled as if he'd slapped her. "The official—?"

Ash leaned back in his chair, shaking his head. "Do you know I had to sit my family down last night and tell them? Can you imagine how devastated they were? Especially Natalie."

He pushed his chair back and stood. He was too angry to stay seated any longer. He walked over to the two-way mirror and watched her reflection.

To his surprise, she was staring at him with a look of confused horror on her face. Was it a distortion of the mirror? He turned. No. She still looked confused.

"Natalie devastated? I'm not sure what you're talking about—" Rachel stopped, biting her lip. She rubbed her temple with two fingers. "Wh-what did you say to them?"

"Come on, Rach, what do you think I said?"

Rachel blinked, and a tear slid down her cheek. She shook her head. "I don't think I und—"

"That's right," he interrupted. "You *didn't* think. You obviously didn't consider what this would do to me. To my family. Why didn't you refuse? I'll bet it was Meeks, wasn't it? I know you've been seeing him. Are you two still tight? Did he talk you into doing it?" She'd dated Tim Meeks, an assistant district attorney, for a few weeks after Ash had delivered his patented *Let's cool things off for a while* spiel. And everybody in the squad knew how ambitious Meeks was.

Rachel swiped at the tear, her eyes narrowing. For the first time she didn't look terrified. He was relieved. Even though he was angry enough at her to spit nails, he hadn't intended to make her cower.

"Tim? Talked me into——?" She looked down at her hands just a second, then back up at him. Gone were the confusion, the horrified expression, even the guilt. In their place was what looked like relief.

"I have no idea what you're talking about," she said archly. "I feel like I walked into the middle of a suspense thriller. Why don't you start at the beginning and tell me just exactly what you *think* I've done, and why you think Tim Meeks talked me into *doing it.*"

Now Ash was confused. But his stoked fury overrode all other emotions. "You know, I have friends in the D.A.'s office, too. My friend was kind enough to give me a heads-up. I appreciated the advance warning. Of course, I'd have appreciated it more coming from you."

"Warning?"

Ash slammed down his palm on the table. "Would you stop acting like you just landed on the planet?" He clenched his jaw. "Rick Campbell——I'm assuming you know who he is?" His voice dripped with sarcasm. "Small-time burglar, loser, slaughtered my parents in their beds twenty years ago?"

Rachel's eyes went wide. She didn't acknowledge his question.

"Is it coming back to you now? His family finally managed to convince District Attorney Jesse Allen to reopen the case and retest the DNA. They're sure that DNA evidence will prove their son didn't murder my parents."

"DNA evidence? Oh, my God."

Ash studied Rachel. Was that surprise or guilt? Of all the terms he might use to describe her, including *dedicated, professional, beautiful, sweet* and *sexy-as-hell,* the words *sneaky, underhanded* or *traitorous* would never come to mind.

"What? Suddenly you remember what you did? Dr. Rachel Stevens, Criminalist, DNA Profiling? It *was* Meeks, wasn't it? He got you to do it. Why didn't you tell me?"

"I didn't—I didn't know," she whispered, her face blanching. The pink spots were gone now. "It was a blind request."

"Right," he retorted. "You expect me to believe—" But Ash didn't get to finish, because Rachel moaned and put her hand over her mouth.

"Oh, no," she mumbled. She shot up out of her chair. "I'm sorry, I'm not feeling well," she muttered as she lurched toward the door.

"Hey, come back here. I need to know the results—" But she was through the door and rushing down the hall, her hand over her mouth.

Ash stared, openmouthed, at her back as she ran from the room.

RACHEL SPLASHED MORE cold water on her face, then let it run over the pulse points in her wrists. She shivered.

Her doctor had told her the nausea usually started at around six weeks. She supposed she was lucky that she'd made it all the way to eight. He'd also told her that with her petite five-foot-three-inch frame, she'd probably be showing in no time.

She turned sideways, let her raincoat slide down her shoulders and arms to the floor and held up the hem of her top. She sucked in her belly and squinted at the mirror. It was a little bit round. And most of it wouldn't suck in. As much as she hated it, the doctor was right.

Another wave of nausea hit her, so she splashed some more water on her face and using her hands as a cup, drank a couple of cold mouthfuls.

Then she patted her face dry, picked up her raincoat and went back to her desk. Under the guise of studying a DNA report that had just hit her desk, she thought about Ash and his accusations.

She'd been sure he was talking about her pregnancy at first, as impossible as that was because she hadn't told anyone yet. But ever since her doctor had confirmed that indeed she was pregnant, she'd felt like she was walking around with a big neon sign over her head.

The longer Ash had railed at her, the more confusing his words were, until he said *Campbell* and *DNA*.

She'd immediately realized what had happened. The knowledge that the DNA she'd run for the police commissioner had belonged to the man who'd murdered Ash's parents had turned her already queasy stomach upside down.

If she'd stayed in the room one second longer, she'd have puked all over the table.

The request, which had come two weeks before, had hardly surprised her. The police commissioner's chief of staff had called her about a special assignment. It was rare to get a request from the top, but it happened. Rachel herself had gotten two previous requests from the commissioner's office.

This request was to run DNA analysis and comparison on a cold case. The commissioner's chief of staff had asked her to pick up the package from the commissioner's office herself.

Of course, she'd been curious when she'd seen the sanitized documents and unlabeled samples, but it wasn't the first time she'd been asked to make an analysis and comparison blind, and she was sure it wouldn't be the last. She'd performed the tests and written her report and, per the commissioner's request, personally delivered the whole packet to his office.

Now she knew which case it was. The Christmas Eve Murders. One of the most widely publicized murders in St. Louis's history. The victims were Joseph and Marie Kendall, beautiful, wealthy and successful. The prominent St. Louis couple had been murdered in their bed on Christmas Eve while their four children, Devin, Ashton, Thaddeus and Natalie, slept peacefully, dreaming of sugarplums, in a nearby wing.

Rachel shuddered as nausea spread through her again. A few deep breaths warded it off. She dug into her purse for a package of crackers and nibbled on one as she processed everything Ash had said.

What surprised her—and hurt her—most was that he actually thought she'd had anything to do with reopening the case. He wasn't thinking clearly, because he knew how her job worked. In the St. Louis Metropolitan Police Department, a not insignificant part of DNA analysis was cold cases.

As a Senior Criminalist #1, DNA Profiling, she processed requests for analysis ranging from appeals from lawyers claiming their clients were falsely imprisoned, to court cases where previous DNA evidence was called into question. Another large part of her job was rechecking and verifying analyses done by outside labs.

She had no control over which cases she reran. She merely delivered on her assignments. Her position was cut-and-dried. She couldn't do favors for anyone if she wanted to.

Ash's accusation that she would have done that kind of favor for Tim Meeks was preposterous. Insulting even.

As if she'd jeopardize her job for the scrawny, preppy A.D.A. She'd gone out with him a time or two after Ash had done what every female in the department had warned her that he would do—wooed her, won her and made her fall in love with him, then dumped her.

The women were right about his legendary charm, too. He'd eased away so cleanly and smoothly that it had hardly hurt—at first.

"So what was that about?" Vanessa asked, twirling her chair around. "I've never seen Ash lose his cool like that. What did you do to him, girl?"

Rachel arched her neck and massaged a knotted muscle there. Then she shook her head and chose her words carefully. "He's upset about a case. He had some questions about the DNA." She hoped the hint that she and Ash were discussing technical DNA questions would quash Vanessa's interest. She was right.

"Oh, okay. I thought you might have managed to make our local Casanova angry. So far Ashanova is batting a thousand. He's the only man I've ever dated that I still like, even after he broke up with me."

Rachel regarded Vanessa. She was dark-haired, pretty and had a fair share of men hanging around. But Ash was in his early thirties while Vanessa couldn't be more than twenty-five. What had he seen in her? Okay, besides the obvious. "How'd he break up with you?"

Vanessa studied her nails. "You know, I'm not sure I can explain it. It just sort of happened."

Rachel nodded. It had just sort of happened with her, too. And Vanessa was right. It was impossible to explain. Somehow, he'd gone from sexy heat to casual cool, and she'd emerged without a scratch—well, except for the baby.

She ran her palm across her tiny baby bump, unable to keep a smile from her face. She was absolutely thrilled about the baby. She was fine with raising it alone. Women did that all the time, and her mother had already been saying for years that she'd be chief babysitter for her future grandkids. And Rachel wasn't worried about providing for her child because she had an extremely well-paying job.

Speaking of which—she needed to get back to it. She moved her mouse to wake her computer. But instead of picking up where she'd left off the day before with a case involving three suspects, all of whom had left their DNA at the crime scene, she went to the search function and pulled up the Christmas Eve Murders case. She paged down to the summary report.

She'd heard of the case, of course. Everyone had. The Kendalls had been prominent on the social and business scenes in St Louis. The tragic story of their murders was embedded into the history of the city.

She skimmed the summary. Now a captain, Charles Hammond had been the lead investigator on the case. Her "uncle" Charlie had been her dad's best friend and fishing buddy until her father was killed in the line of duty.

She continued reading. An ex-con named Richard Campbell had been arrested skulking around the upscale neighborhood of Hortense Place where the Kendalls lived, on that Christmas Eve twenty years before.

In a statement to the press, then-Detective Hammond had reported that Campbell had two previous convictions for burglary. He'd been out on bail when the murders occurred. Based on Campbell's rap sheet and the preliminary investigation, Hammond said the murders appeared to be impulsive rather than premeditated, perhaps a robbery gone bad.

An eyewitness placed Campbell close to the Kendall

estate that evening, carrying jewelry and rare coins, later found to be from nearby houses he'd broken into.

Rachel read another couple of paragraphs but the only additional bit of evidence mentioned was that Campbell had scratches on his right arm and Marie Kendall had tissue and blood under her fingernails.

Of course Campbell swore he was innocent and also that the scratches had happened as he had crawled out the window of the last house he'd burglarized.

"Didn't anyone check the window for blood?" she muttered. She'd need to pull the case file to check on that, and she was pretty sure she wouldn't be granted access to it, not now.

She took another tiny bite of cracker as she double-checked the date of the murders. She shook her head. Twenty years ago DNA profiling was in its infancy—newborn in fact. The vast storehouse of specific identification information that Rachel took for granted hadn't even been dreamed of when the Kendalls were killed.

But damning circumstantial evidence plus public outrage over the cold-blooded murder of a prominent St. Louis couple had resulted in a quick conviction. Campbell had received two consecutive life sentences.

Dear God. Rachel sat back in her chair, her hand over her mouth. Now, DNA had exonerated Rick Campbell. Twenty years ago, not one but two families had been destroyed—the Kendalls and the Campbells. Now, one family, the Campbells, was healed—scarred but healed, while the other, Ash's family, was being destroyed all over again.

"What?" Vanessa said, turning toward her.

Rachel started. Had she spoken aloud? "What? Oh, nothing. Sorry. Talking to myself."

Vanessa looked at her oddly. "Okay," she said, and turned back to her computer.

Rachel leaned her elbows on her desk and covered her face with her hands. What was she going to do? She thought about the report she'd sent to the police commissioner, especially her conclusions. The last line of her conclusion appeared emblazoned on her eyelids, as she reviewed the last paragraph in her mind.

The DNA analysis of Sample 90-12-335 yields a 99.9935% probability that the tissue, blood and hair samples found at the scene belong to the same individual. These samples, compared to the submitted sample, 11-09-125, yield only a 0.0000003% match. Conclusion: The samples found at the crime scene and the submitted sample do not match. The two sets of DNA are distinctive and belong to two different people.

I'm so sorry, Ash, she said silently. *So very sorry.* How was she ever going to face him again? She was already carrying one secret that would change his life forever. Now she had a second. Within days, he and his family would know that Rick Campbell, who'd served twenty years for the murder of Joseph and Marie Kendall, was irrefutably innocent. The real murderer was walking around free.

Chapter Two

Late that afternoon, Rachel stood in the living room of Ash's two-bedroom house for the first time in two months, trying not to cry. She was still devastated about the DNA analysis, and hyperemotional anyway, because of her pregnancy. Then, just as she'd been about to leave for the day, Ash had stopped by her desk and told her—no, *ordered* her—to pick up the last of her things from his house, and leave the key he'd given her.

So here she was, where some of the best times of her life had taken place. Ash was the sexiest, funniest, sweetest and most charming man she'd ever known. The passion between them had flared like a supernova and had never dimmed. At least hers hadn't.

Her friends at work had warned her about him. Behind his back they called him *Ashanova* and joked that his motto was *love 'em and leave 'em—happy.*

She'd of course thought she was different. And she was—at least in one way. As far as she knew, none of the other women he'd dated had ended up pregnant.

Her hand drifted to her tummy and she smiled through the tears that streamed down her cheeks. This little baby was an accident, although Rachel would never tell him or her. Sadly, on her part, this baby had been conceived in love. Too bad the father had just been having fun.

She brushed away the tears from her cheeks and surveyed Ash's normally neat house. It was a mess. Half a pizza sat congealing on the coffee table, along with a couple of empty beer cans. She glanced into his bedroom. The covers were piled on the floor and two empty glasses sat on the nightstand. A pile of dirty clothes lay in the doorway to the bathroom.

He hadn't slept a wink the night before. If she hadn't already confirmed it by the circles under his eyes, she knew it now. Looking at his rumpled bed, she could picture him tossing and turning as he tried to shut out visions of his slaughtered parents.

And she couldn't even blame him for his anger. His whole life—and the lives of his family—had just been toppled like Humpty Dumpty. He'd gone through the horror of losing his parents twenty years ago. Now, he had to face a new horror, an even more devastating one. Whoever had killed his parents was still out there—free.

But even if she'd known whose DNA she was comparing, it wouldn't have made a difference. She had an obligation to the victims, to the department, and yes, even to the suspects, to not only uncover the truth, but to keep the information confidential.

She debated for a second whether to make his bed and straighten up, then immediately thought better of it. He'd probably think she was trying to get back in his good graces. Her best bet was to pick up her things and get out before he got home.

Her things. What had she left here anyway? She hadn't moved in with him, so anything she'd left had been accidental. Sort of.

She shook her head in frustration as she looked in the medicine cabinet in the bathroom and found a soft-bristle toothbrush and a hair clip. In the nightstand she discovered her favorite watch, and on his dresser was a gold hoop earring she'd been sure she'd lost.

Had she subconsciously left these things here in hopes of reminding him of their passionate nights and the weekends they'd spent making love, sleeping, eating, watching a ball game or a movie and then making love some more? She couldn't really deny it.

She stowed the few belongings in her purse and headed toward the front door. As soon as she crossed the threshold into the living room, the smell of the leftover pizza sent nausea crawling up her throat again. Holding her breath, she hurried into the kitchen and ran a glass of cold water from the refrigerator door dispenser and leaned against the counter, sipping it.

The cold liquid cooled her throat and lessened the nausea a little bit. But when she straightened, stars danced in front of her eyes and her head felt woozy. She knew the signs. Ever since she was little, those stars had preceded light-headedness and, if she didn't sit or lie down immediately, fainting. She hoped she wasn't going to see stars her entire pregnancy.

She took the water over to the kitchen table and sat down. She rolled the cold plastic against her forehead, hoping to clear her head and stop the dizziness. But the stars got brighter. So she rested her forehead on her folded arms—just for a minute, until the queasiness dissipated. Then she had to get out of here.

It wouldn't be a good idea to be here when Ash got home.

ASH HAD JUST COME OUT of the grocery store when his phone rang.

"Hey," a familiar voice said.

"Thaddeus, little brother. Thank God. I figured I wouldn't hear from you for a week—or a month."

"Well, the words *family emergency* sort of cut through the usual red tape. What's going on? Is everyone all right?"

"Red tape? Are you embedded with the troops somewhere?" Thad was a photojournalist with a renowned news magazine, not a special agent. How much red tape could there be?

There was a brief pause, then Thad spoke. "Figure of speech," he said. "So what's the emergency? Is everybody okay?"

"Everybody's okay, but I've got some bad news."

"What?" Thad's voice sharpened.

"The new D.A. here accepted the Campbell family's petition to have Campbell's DNA run against the blood and tissue they found under Mom's fingernails."

"The DNA?" Thad repeated. After a short pause he asked, "Well, it's Campbell's, right? I mean, it has to be."

"I haven't seen the results. I'm not even supposed to know about it."

"Your girlfriend, the criminalist, tell you?" Thad knew about Rachel. Whenever he and Ash talked, he always asked who the new flame was and, feeling sorry for his brother, so far away from home and stuck taking pictures of death and devastation in one war-torn country or another, Ash always told him. But they hadn't talked since he'd broken up with her.

"Ex-girlfriend, and she's the one who ran the analysis," Ash said bitterly as he tossed the grocery bags in the backseat of his car and got in the driver's seat.

"Damn. That stings. Still, she's the criminalist, right? So it's her job. Have you told everybody? Or are you waiting for the results?"

Not for the first time, Ash questioned his judgment in

letting his aunt and uncle, his brothers and his baby sister know about the petition. Should he have waited for the results to come back? "I told 'em. Maybe I shouldn't have."

"How'd they take it? How's Natalie?"

"Terrified. What would you expect?"

"Did the news trigger anything? Did she remember something?"

"No, I'm pretty sure it didn't. She doesn't seem to remember finding Mom and Dad at all. All she knows is what she's been told about that morning."

"Still—I guess she was pretty shaken up?"

"Yeah. I told her that she ought to see the shrink at Kendall Communications, but she still refuses."

"I can't blame her. I'm not so sure it would be a good idea for her to remember what she saw. I wish I didn't have that picture in my head, and I was five years older than Nat. What about the others? Devin?"

"He's sure the DNA will come back as Campbell's, just like I am. Aunt Angie is just worried about all of us, but man—you should have seen Uncle Craig. I thought he was going to have a stroke, right there. I nearly had to wrestle him to the ground to keep him from calling the D.A."

"Well, Dad was his brother."

"Yeah, but his reaction was way over-the-top. His face turned purple and he had trouble breathing. Seriously, I thought he was going to stroke out on me."

"But he's okay?"

"Yeah. For now."

"Ash, what if the DNA doesn't match?" Thad asked.

Ash winced as if dodging a bullet that had struck too close for comfort. "It'll match," he said starkly.

"Right. But what if it doesn't?"

Ash's shoulders hunched against the question. "I don't

know. Hell, it's been twenty years. I can't even imagine that it won't."

He heard Thad sigh through the phone. "I know. But I don't like what my gut's telling me. Listen. I think I can break away. I'll let you know when I can be there."

"You don't have to do that. There's nothing you can do to change anything. I just thought you ought to know what's going on."

"Nope. I've decided. I'm due some time off. I'll just need to clear it and then find a plane to hitch a ride on. That could take a while. I might end up having to ride with cargo. But I'll let you know as soon as I can."

"Great. It'll be good to see you."

"Hang on a minute," Thad said. "You're not getting away that easy. If Rachel's status is now ex—big surprise—then who's the latest flame?"

Ash grimaced. "There's not one at the moment."

"Not one? You've got to be kidding me. What? Did you two break up *yesterday?*"

"No. Two months ago."

"Okay. First, I'm seriously impressed that you remember how long it's been, and second—two months! That's got to be a record. What's the matter with you?"

"Maybe I'm taking a break," Ash said wryly.

"Maybe." Thad's voice had changed. Ash would swear his younger brother was grinning. "And maybe you're still hung up on her."

Ash winced. "No. I don't *get* hung up."

"There's always a first time, even for Ashton Kendall, confirmed ladies' man."

"Say goodbye, Thad," Ash muttered.

"Goodbye, Thad."

Ash hung up and headed for his house, frowning as he replayed his and Thad's conversation in his head. Thad

had always been able to read him. There was some truth
to what he'd said. Ash hadn't dated anyone since he had
broken up with Rachel. He considered his brother's comment and his own response. Of course he didn't get hung
up. But Rachel was the singularly most irritating woman
he'd ever dated. Irritating and interesting.

He shook off those thoughts and concentrated on Thad's
other irritating quality—his ability to drill down to the
heart of any situation. Thad's other question replayed in
his mind, the same question that had bothered him ever
since he'd heard the news.

The question no one else in the family had asked—not
Devin, not Aunt Angie or Uncle Craig and not Natalie.

What if the DNA didn't match? What if Rick Campbell
was innocent?

As Ash turned onto his street, he saw Rachel's car in his
driveway. He looked at his watch. Six-thirty. Damn it. She
got off at five. She'd had plenty of time to get here, clear
out her stuff and leave.

It wasn't like he wasn't already haunted by the ghost of
her presence in his home, in his bed—a new experience
for him. One he didn't like. Did she think seeing her in his
house would land them back in the sack? At that thought,
his body tightened in immediate sexual response.

No! No way. He had let her down gently and moved on,
same as always. He loved women, but he wasn't interested
in settling down. Ever.

He'd heard the talk. He knew what people—and by
people he meant women—said about him.

Love 'em and leave 'em—happy. It was true. The phrase
summed up his attitude toward women in a nutshell. But
since Rachel, he hadn't found anyone he was interested in
enough to ask out.

For a split second he considered turning around and leaving. Give her plenty of time to clear out. He could run over to the mansion, not to see his aunt and uncle, but to check on Natalie, who had moved into the roomy guest cottage a couple of years ago. He wanted to make sure she was doing okay.

Then his stubborn streak kicked in. This was his home. He wasn't the one who should be leaving. Rachel was. He pulled up to the curb, leaving the driveway clear behind Rachel's car.

Stalking inside, he stopped short when he didn't see her. Not in the living room and not in his bedroom. But what he did see took him aback.

Damn, he'd left a mess. He'd had trouble falling asleep, ordered a pizza at midnight that he'd barely touched and then finally drifted into a fitful sleep around four-thirty. He took a deep breath and wrinkled his nose at the smell of cold, stale tomato sauce and cheese. He didn't mind cold pizza, but he liked it from the refrigerator, not sitting out all day.

He picked up the pizza box and took it into the kitchen to throw into the trash. He stopped cold. Rachel was sitting at the kitchen table, her head on her hands, asleep.

"Rach, what the hell are you doing?"

She started, then lifted her head. There was a red patch on her left cheek where it had rested on her hand. "Wha—?" She blinked. "Oh, Ash. I'm sorry. I didn't mean to fall asleep."

Ash found himself caught by her eyes. He wasn't sure what it was about those gold-green eyes with the reddish-brown ring around the edge of the iris, but he did know they had the power to make him think crazy thoughts—like how great it would be to fall into bed with her again, or how at thirty-three he was getting a little tired of the chase. How his flirtatious lifestyle wasn't so much exciting these days as exhausting.

He shook his head to dislodge those thoughts that had been creeping into his mind ever since he'd cooled it between them. He had no intentions of changing anything about his lifestyle—which was why he wanted Rachel's stuff out of here. He never brought women to his house and this was why.

Invariably, once a woman got a toe in the door, she started nesting—leaving things in his bathroom, his bedroom, sometimes even in his bed.

Plus, he didn't like the silly twinge that squeezed his chest every time he opened his medicine cabinet and saw Rachel's toothbrush.

"Well, you're awake now," he said ungraciously. "Did you get all your stuff?"

She nodded and stood, closing her eyes for a couple of seconds. She was pale as she picked up her purse. "I hope you don't mind, I got—some water," she said, sounding slightly out of breath.

Ash frowned. What was wrong with her? Was she upset that he'd told her to come and clear her stuff out of his house? He was the one who had a right to be upset, not her.

She stepped past him into the living room, muttering something that he didn't catch.

"What?" he asked, following her.

She shook her head. "Nothing," she muttered. "Nothing." She hurried toward the door.

"Rach, wait a minute."

She stopped without turning around.

"We never got to finish our conversation this morning."

She turned. The red patch on her cheek stood out against her pale skin. "You call that a conversation? I'd call it an interrogation. You were really at the top of your game."

Ash shrugged. He wasn't happy with the way he'd acted, although for the most part, he felt like it was justified. Okay, maybe not slapping the table. "Why didn't you give me the courtesy of letting me know you were running the DNA found on my parents' bodies?"

"Come on, Ash," Rachel said, sounding exasperated. "I didn't know whose sample it was. It was a special request, with a one-day turnaround. Everything that could possibly point to a particular case had been redacted. You know how they do those things."

"You should have known by the date," he snapped. "How many twenty-year-old Christmas Eve murder cases do you think there have been in St. Louis?"

She leaned her head back against the front door and closed her eyes. "The date was redacted, too."

"How about the fact that there were two victims, or—"

"Please, Ash. Even if I should have known, I didn't," she said, bringing her gaze to his. "Even if I had realized whose case it was, I couldn't have told you. You know that. And this case was more sensitive than most. It was specially requested by the commissioner."

"The commissioner?" Ash was shocked. It was the police commissioner who had granted the petition to reopen the case and have the DNA sampled, not the new D.A.?

Ash felt like he'd taken a blow to the stomach. His own boss hadn't given him the courtesy of a heads-up. That stung.

Rachel was watching him closely. He shut his eyes for an instant, composing his thoughts and blocking the look on her face. She obviously hadn't meant to say that much, because her lips were pressed together tightly.

"You're sure? It wasn't the D.A.?" he asked, even though he knew he hadn't misunderstood.

"I can't talk about this," she protested. "I'm—I need to go."

Her voice sounded strained, more strained than it should have, given their conversation. He wasn't about to let her leave until he had all the answers he needed. "No. Not yet. What did you find? What were the results?"

Rachel turned the knob on the door, but her fingers slipped. "I—can't—"

He stepped toward her. "Rachel, did the DNA match? This is my parents' murder we're talking about. I need to know!" he demanded.

"Ash, stop it. You know I can't tell you anything."

"This is me," he said, thumping his chest. "I was asleep down the hall while that man murdered my mom and dad. My baby sister found them on Christmas morning. She was six years old. *Six.* Can't you understand what this means to me—to my family?"

He was so close to her now that he could see sweat beading on her forehead. Her face had lost all its color, and her lips were pinched so tightly together that their corners were bluish-white.

"Rach?"

"I—can't," she gasped. "I just can't—" She turned and tried again to twist the knob and open the door. But her fingers slid off.

"Ash—?" she whispered. "Help—"

And she collapsed.

Chapter Three

By the time they got to the hospital, Rachel was alert and begging the EMTs to let her go home. But to Ash's relief they didn't pay the least bit of attention to her.

She'd only been unconscious for a few minutes, but it was long enough to scare the spit out of him. One second she'd been turning the knob on his front door and the next, she'd collapsed directly into his arms. He'd lowered her gently to the floor and made sure she was breathing, then he'd tried to wake her, but she'd been out cold.

He'd called 9–1–1 and identified himself as a detective with the Ninth District of the St. Louis Metropolitan Police Department, and ordered an ambulance.

By the time he'd hung up, Rachel had stirred. But she was nearly incoherent, so he'd made her stay on the floor and cradled her head until the EMTs got there.

Now he was pacing the waiting room floor like an expectant father as he waited for the doctor to finish examining her. They'd probably run a bunch of tests. Hell, they could be here until midnight.

A woman—who'd been sitting in the waiting room knitting ever since the nurse had deposited him in this drab little room that smelled of old coffee—looked up at him. "Your wife?" she asked.

Ash stared at her for a second, uncomprehending. "Uh, no. A coworker."

"A coworker?" the woman said meaningfully, then she held his gaze until he relented.

"And you?"

"My son," she said. "He came home tonight with a bloody nose. He got into a fight."

"It's broken? How old is he?"

She nodded with a sigh. "He's thirteen. Old enough to know better, but not old enough to restrain himself."

Just then a nurse appeared in the doorway. Ash and the woman both turned to her.

"Mr. Kendall?"

He stepped forward.

"Ms. Stevens is ready to go. You can follow me."

"What happened? Is she okay?"

The nurse gave him an odd, knowing look. "I'll let her tell you all about it."

The nurse led him to a cubicle and slid the curtain back. "Here you go, Ms. Stevens. I'll send the aide with the wheelchair."

"I don't need a wheelchair."

The nurse looked at Ash, who nodded, then turned back to Rachel. "Oh, I think you do. We don't want to take a chance that you might faint again."

Ash felt a jolt of relief to see that Rachel had color in her cheeks. She looked a hundred percent better than she had when he'd brought her in.

"You look like a different person," he said. "What did the doctor say?"

Rachel busied herself with her purse. "My blood sugar was low."

"That's all? You passed out because you hadn't eaten?"

Ash's anger rose again, this time because he knew she was lying. Her answer had been too quick, too flip.

"That's not *exactly* how low blood sugar works," she retorted, "but basically, I guess you could say that." She wouldn't look at him, just kept rummaging in her purse until the aide came with the wheelchair.

She was definitely hiding something. A sudden thought sent a pang of fear arrowing into his gut. Was something wrong with her? Something serious? No, that wasn't it. The nurse hadn't seemed worried or sad. She'd seemed more—secretive, as if she knew something he didn't know.

The aide kept up a stream of conversation, or more accurately, prattle, all the way to the emergency entrance. As the wheelchair turned the corner a few steps ahead of Ash, he heard a deep voice call Rachel's name.

He turned the corner in time to see that the owner of the voice was in a white lab coat with a stethoscope around his neck. He was shaking Rachel's hand.

"—and congratulations," he said with a smile before he hurried away.

Congratulations? Why would any doctor say that to a patient?

He thought back to the nurse's secretive look.

Oh, hell. Ash could think of only one reason for the medical staff's reactions, and that reason sent lightning bolts of shock all the way to his toes.

There weren't many things Ashton Kendall was afraid of. He'd discovered on that fateful Christmas Eve so long ago that life was too short to spend it in fear.

He'd transformed the grief and fear that he'd learned way too young into fierce determination. He'd turned the helplessness and anger into a hunger for justice and a career. And finally, he'd filled the empty place in his heart with a casual, carefree charm that earned him lots of dates and friends without getting him into an emotional tangle.

But he wasn't sure if he could face what he'd just been hit with.

Was he about to become a father?

RACHEL'S HAND FELT NUMB where the doctor had shaken it, but it was not as numb as her heart. She waited without breathing to see what Ash was going to say. She knew he'd heard the doctor because she could feel his gaze boring into her back. Besides, she didn't dare look at him. If he hadn't already figured out what the doctor had meant by his congratulations, he'd see it written all over her face.

About that time, he walked past the wheelchair.

"I'll get the car," he said shortly as he stalked toward the elevators without looking back. He sounded just like he had when he'd found her asleep in his house.

Downstairs, he helped her into the car with an offhand gentleness that confused her. And he didn't say anything on the drive back to his house, where her car was still parked in his driveway. But he kept glancing over at her, a bemused expression on his face.

Once he'd pulled to the curb and parked, he turned toward her. "I guess congratulations are in order," he said evenly.

Here it came. Rachel bit her bottom lip and stared at her hands, which were clasped in her lap. His words hovered in the air, demanding an explanation.

"So that's why you fainted?" he went on. "You're pregnant." His voice sounded strained. "Why did you think you had to lie to me about the low blood sugar?"

She squeezed her interlaced fingers together. "It wasn't a lie exactly. I've always had problems with low blood sugar."

He didn't say anything for a moment. He just looked at her. "So how far along are you?"

Her head snapped up. "Checking the time frame?" she asked bitterly.

He shrugged and dropped his gaze. His jaw quivered with tension.

"I'm eight weeks pregnant. My ob-gyn told me I probably conceived around the last week in July. His guess is July 22." She threw the date down as a challenge and waited to see what Ash said.

He knew as well as she did the exact date he'd broached the subject of seeing other people. She'd never been a maudlin person, but that date was branded on her brain. It had been Saturday, August 7, two weeks after their honeymoon-like trip to New Orleans. He'd couched the conversation in terms of friends talking about what they had planned for the fall, but Rachel had recognized it for what it was—the casual, charming brush-off. It had been nine days later when she'd realized she was pregnant.

Now she met his gaze. "But in case you're wondering, I didn't rush out and find myself a new man the next day. In fact, I haven't found one at all."

"That's not what I meant—"

"Look, Ash, I have no intention of making demands on you. I'm choosing to have this baby and it's my decision and mine alone. You don't have to worry about that."

"Listen to me. If it's my baby, then I will take responsibility for it."

Rachel didn't hear what he said after the word *if.* She stiffened. "If?" she repeated. "If? You don't believe me?" There came the tears, clawing their way up from her throat. She swallowed hard. "Well, that makes all of this easier."

She opened the passenger door and got out. She felt Ash's hand brush her elbow.

"Rach, wait. Of course I believe—"

But she kept going. Right to her car. She climbed in, started the engine and backed out of the driveway. When she turned the corner, heading toward her own apartment, Ash was still sitting in his car at the curb.

ASH DOUBLED HIS FIST and took a swing at the steering wheel. His hand stung, but luckily, his car was sturdy enough to withstand the blow.

Idiot! How in hell had he let Rachel get pregnant? Of course before the question even formed, he knew the answer. He remembered it as if it were yesterday. Friday, July 22. They'd flown down to New Orleans for the weekend. They'd had a couple of Hurricanes, the deceptively sweet drink so popular on Bourbon Street. They'd gone back to the hotel and made love—a lot.

When Ash had woken up the next morning, he'd vaguely remembered rolling over deep in the night and coaxing Rachel awake. They'd done it two more times. It had been spontaneous and satisfying and—he now knew for sure— without benefit of protection.

He cranked the car and drove to the mansion, bypassing it and heading straight for the guesthouse, where Natalie lived. On the way he called her and asked if she was decent.

Natalie had on a black T-shirt and drawstring pants with red chili peppers on them. She'd twisted up her long blond hair into a knot.

He kissed the top of her head as he stepped inside. "How're you doing?" he asked.

She preceded him into her small living room and flopped onto her couch, her legs crossed beneath her. She was drinking something red.

"Cranberry juice," she said. "Want some?"

He shook his head and sat in a chair next to the couch.

"I'm doing okay, Ash. Better than I thought I would be."

He assessed her. "You sure, squirt? Because you look tired."

"Thanks." She laughed. "I didn't sleep well last night. My brain wouldn't stop whirling."

"I know what you mean. Our brains were probably whirling in unison. Bad dreams?"

Natalie looked down at the glass in her hand. "No. Not really. Just couldn't get to sleep."

"Have you thought any more about seeing the company psychiatrist?"

Natalie's pleasant expression darkened. "I really wish you'd drop that idea," she said. "I am fine. If you just came over here to bully me, you can show yourself out."

"Apparently this is the week for surprises. I got some weird news tonight."

"Weird? What do you mean, weird?"

He took a deep breath, opened his mouth and closed it again.

Natalie watched him, a small frown wrinkling her forehead. "Okay, Ashton, spit it out," she snapped—her version of encouraging and sympathetic.

He smiled wryly. "Rachel—Rachel Stevens—is pregnant."

To his surprise, Natalie's mouth didn't drop open in shock. In fact, while her expression at first reflected surprise, it morphed quickly to thoughtfulness to what he could only describe as sheer joy.

"Wow!" she exclaimed. "My first niece—or nephew. Good job!" She leaned forward, her right hand in the air. Did she really think he felt like high-fiving her over this?

He closed his eyes and shook his head. "Nat—"

She pulled back her hand but her enthusiasm didn't dampen. "This is the best news I've heard in a while. I'm going to be an aunt!"

He scowled at her.

"And look," she said, gesturing at him. "Talk about irony. The Kendall playboy is the first to fall. Congrats! Have you told Dev or Aunt Angela?"

"Nat, stop it! This is not something I want to tell anybody. For sure not Aunt Angie. It is *not* a good thing. Be serious, would you?"

Natalie beamed at him. "I am being serious. This is *seriously* fabulous news. Are you getting married right away?"

"No!"

When he saw the shock on Natalie's face, he realized how loud and sharp his answer had been. "I'm sorry, but I just found out not even an hour ago, and I'm not sure what I'm going to do about it."

"Do about it? You think you're going to *do* something about it? Unless by *do something* you mean ask Rachel to marry you and buy a house and get ready to be a husband and a father, I can tell you right now, there's nothing you can do about it."

Ash leaned forward, planting his elbows on his knees and running his fingers through his hair. He sat there, palms cradling his head. "Tell me about it. But, Nat, I have never been careless. Ever."

Natalie frowned at him, her head cocked to one side. "Come on, Ash. Haven't we had this conversation? Not even condoms are one-hundred-percent effective."

He stared at her. "I know that, but—"

For a short moment, Natalie held his gaze. Then she stood. "But what? Do you think the baby's not yours?"

He blew out a breath between his teeth. "Oh, I know

it's mine. Rachel wouldn't lie. Plus, I know exactly when it happened."

"Great. So when are you two—you three—getting married?" Natalie grinned at him.

Ash sat up, rubbed the spot on his chest where the hollow feeling resided. He clamped his jaw and forced his mind away from the confusing question of how he felt about Rachel.

"There's another issue," he muttered. He wiped his face and looked up at her. "Rachel's the one who ran the DNA."

Natalie looked puzzled. "The baby's DNA?"

"No, no," he said, leaning forward and again propping his elbows on his knees. "She's the one who ran the samples from the murders against Campbell's DNA."

Natalie's initial reaction was shock. The color drained from her face. She was quiet for a second, staring past him at nothing in particular. Then her gaze returned to his. "That's her job, isn't it? I mean, doesn't she run all the DNA tests? Did she know whose it was?"

"She says no. She says the paperwork that came with the samples was redacted. But she should have known. It's not like St. Louis has had that many double murders."

"Well, that's true. Wow." Natalie was quiet for another moment. Then she leaned forward. "She didn't say anything about the results, did she?"

"Nope. Not a word." Ash studied his younger sister. "I'm sorry, Nat. I didn't want to upset you, but I thought you should know. I know you like Rachel."

"I do. Better than most of the women you've dated. She's a really good person. All that and gorgeous, too. Your baby is going to be a knockout."

Ash groaned.

Natalie drank the rest of her juice and headed toward the kitchen. At the door she turned around, frowning and rubbing her forehead. "What's really bothering you, Ash? From what I know of Rachel, she's honest and kind and good at her job. I don't know a lot about DNA, but from what I understand, it's pretty specific. Either the DNA is Rick Campbell's or it isn't."

She set down her glass, propped her fists on her hips and cocked her head. "You have no idea what's wrong with you, do you?"

Ash spread his hands. "With me? What are you talking about?"

She stalked over to stand directly in front of him. "Come on, Ashton. It's so obvious. Ash Kendall—Ashanova—" she held up her hands as if displaying headlines "—finally hoisted by his own petard."

He stood, shaking his head and digging his car keys from his pocket. "You're not making any sense. I'd better go. I just wanted to see how you were doing."

"Liar. You wanted me to tell you that everything is all Rachel's fault. Well, I won't. You can't turn and walk away from her like you have every other woman you've dated."

"I'm not planning to. I'll provide for the baby."

Natalie poked a finger into the middle of his chest. "You'll do more than that. You might as well accept it. Rachel's different, and not because of the baby. You're in love with her. Everybody knows it. We've just been waiting for you to figure it out."

"You're nuts," he said with a laugh that sounded more like a cough. "I'm *not* in love with her, and you'd better not say a word about this to anyone, especially not Aunt Angie and Uncle Craig. They're upset enough as it is."

"I won't."

"Swear?"

Natalie held up her right hand. "Swear. It's going to be fun to watch you squirm. Because sooner or later it's going to dawn on you that you haven't stopped thinking about Rachel since the moment you first noticed her."

Ash ignored her and headed for the door. He turned back. "Nat, you're sure you're all right?"

She nodded and smiled. "I'm fine. Thanks for taking care of me. Ash?"

"Yeah?"

"What happens now?"

He wasn't sure which shocking event she was talking about—Rachel's pregnancy or the reanalysis of the DNA.

"I mean, if Rick Campbell didn't do it."

He shrugged and let out a long breath. "Then I guess I'm going to have to find the man who did kill our parents."

Chapter Four

By the next afternoon, Ash was sick of hearing Natalie's voice in his head. *You're in love with her.* He wasn't. He couldn't be. He didn't fall in love. He had fun, sure, and he did love women. But there was no place in his life for a family. He'd decided a long time ago that he didn't believe in forever.

"Okay, okay," he muttered in a last-ditch effort to shut up Natalie's nagging voice. "I'm working on a plan." He'd start by apologizing to Rachel for being a jerk about her pregnancy and officially offer his help with raising the baby. He'd provide for the child's rearing and education. And if Rachel agreed, he wanted to be a part of his son's or daughter's life.

He'd woken in the middle of the night and discovered, to his surprise, that he wanted his child to know him. He knew Rachel would eventually get married. But she wouldn't refuse to let him see his child—would she?

He'd tried to call her but she hadn't answered, so he'd gone over to her apartment. As he stepped up to the door, he noticed it wasn't locked. It swung inward a fraction of an inch. He frowned. It wasn't like Rachel to leave her door open. Then he saw the splintered wood on the far side of the door facing.

Rachel! Someone had broken the door in. Adrenaline

surged through him, upping his heart rate and tensing his muscles in fight-or-flight response.

He instinctively rose to the balls of his feet as he glanced around at the other three doors off this breezeway, then pulled his Sig Sauer from the paddle holster at the small of his back.

For two seconds, he stood perfectly still, taking deep, long breaths, working to calm his pounding heart. Then he held his gun in his right hand, his left supporting it, took one more deep breath and angled around the door. The sight before him ratcheted up his racing pulse. Rachel's living room had been turned upside down.

He eased forward, his gun held at the ready, as he took in the tossed couch cushions, DVDs scattered on the carpet, chairs overturned. Where was she? Was she hurt?

He didn't dare call out until he'd cleared the apartment. He moved across the room to check the bedroom. It was a mess, too, mattresses on the floor, bedclothes scattered, drawers ransacked. But no sign of an intruder.

"Clear," he whispered, glancing into the bathroom. Crossing to the kitchen, he eased around the door facing and saw Rachel.

She was sprawled on the floor, dark blood staining the crown of her head.

The sight sheared his breath. Only his strict military training and crime scene experience kept him from rushing to her side until he'd verified that there was no one else here. He checked the back door. Locked—a double dead bolt.

Then he crouched down beside Rachel. She was breathing. Relief doused him like cold water.

"Rach, wake up." He put out a shaky hand. "It's Ash. Are you okay?" The dark blood in her matted hair was wet and shiny. It had started to ooze down her neck and drip onto the floor.

She stirred, moaning. "Ash?" she muttered. "My head—" She moved to sit up, but he stopped her.

"Careful," he said. "You're bleeding from your scalp. Does anything else hurt?"

She turned her head so she could see him, and grimaced. "No. Maybe my knee. He pushed me down." She got her hands under her and pushed. "Let me sit up," she demanded.

"Just wait a second. I don't know if you should move. What about—?" He reached out toward her stomach. "What about the baby?"

Rachel's head snapped up and her golden eyes searched his. "The baby's fine," she said. "But I need to sit up."

He helped her. When she did, he saw her keys on the floor under her.

She moaned a little, grimaced and then relaxed. She touched her head. Her hand came away stained with blood. "Oh," she gasped.

Her pain, shock and especially fear rekindled Ash's anger—not toward her this time but on her behalf. His hand tightened on the gun and his vision darkened. Whoever had hurt her would have to answer to him.

"How long has he been gone?" he asked as the urge to give chase tightened his leg muscles.

"I'm not sure—maybe five minutes."

"Damn it." Ash considered running outside to see if he saw anyone suspicious, but he'd already been here three or four minutes. The man was long gone by now.

She touched her head again. "I was afraid to move. Afraid he'd hit me again or kill me. When I first heard your footsteps, I thought he'd come back."

"You're sure it was a man?"

She nodded gingerly. "I could tell by his voice."

"His voice? What did he say?"

"Nothing to me. He was muttering to himself and cursing."

"Did you get a look at his face?"

"No."

"His build? Complexion? Clothes?"

"I—don't know." Her gaze met his, wide-eyed, worried. "I'm sorry."

"Hey, it's okay. How are you feeling? No other pains? Are you sure—?" He stopped, his voice strangled by an odd tightening in his chest. He cleared his throat. "Are you sure the baby's okay?"

Her fingers spread across her tummy and she met his gaze. Her brow furrowed slightly as she shook her head. "I didn't hit my stomach or land on it. I'm sure the baby's fine."

"Turn your head. Let me look at that cut," Ash told her. He examined the wound closely. "How badly does it hurt?" he asked.

"Just kind of throbs and stings a little."

"I don't think it's more than a cut. Scalp wounds bleed like crazy." He took out his phone. "But I'm going to call an ambulance anyhow."

"No," she said emphatically.

"Sorry, standard procedure." He dialed. "This is Detective Ash Kendall. I've got a home invasion with injuries," he said and gave the address. "And send an ambulance."

Rachel's hazel eyes sparked with anger. "You're getting an ambulance out here to bandage a cut on my head?"

He shrugged. "Like I said, standard procedure. They'll check you out and issue an official report of your injuries. Don't worry about it. Here, let me help you up."

He took her hands and helped her to her feet, then

guided her to a chair. She seemed so small. His anger at whoever had done this flared again.

He sat across from her, watching her closely. Her eyes weren't dilated and she looked directly at him, so she wasn't having trouble focusing. At least she didn't have a concussion. "Tell me what happened."

"I'd just lain down for a nap when I heard something. Like wood splintering. I realized someone had broken in the front door. I grabbed my keys and tried to run out the back door, but—" She paused and shuddered. "He grabbed me from behind and hit me on the head."

"With what?" Ash asked.

"I don't know. It hurt. I guess I was knocked out for a while, but I could hear him throwing things around and cursing."

Ash glanced back toward the kitchen. "He didn't go out the back," he said.

"No. It's a double dead bolt, and I guess I fell on top of my keys. He had to have gone out the front."

Sirens sounded in the distance. "They'll be here any minute," he said. "As soon as the EMTs are done with you and the detectives question you, I'll get you out of here."

"No. The way it sounded, he tore up everything. I need to put things back."

Ash stood and held out his hand. "You won't be cleaning in here for a while."

"What about my clothes?" she asked.

"Not 'til CSI gets through. You know the drill."

Her face shut down. She nodded. "Do you think I could have a drink of water?"

Ash smiled at her. "I think we could manage that." He filled a glass from the cold water dispenser on her refrigerator and handed it to her. She sipped it carefully, trying not to tilt her head much.

He sat at the table across from her. There was dark, dried blood on her neck and occasionally she'd brush at it with her fingertips.

Ash closed his eyes and took a deep breath. The sight of the dried blood catapulted him back twenty years, just as it did every time he worked a violent crime, to the morning he'd woken to hear Natalie's screams. He'd worked dozens of murders and assaults in his eight years on the job, and every one of them evoked that awful morning.

He'd been thirteen, too young to have prevented his parents' deaths, but old enough to feel guilty that he hadn't. Time and wisdom had allowed him to forgive himself.

After all, the kids' rooms had been in a separate wing of the mansion. The police had said that if their bedrooms had been near their parents' room, they all might have been killed.

Ash knew himself well enough to know that he'd chosen law enforcement as a way to make up for not saving his parents. Every time he collared a murderer, he felt a little less empty, a little less damaged by his mom and dad's violent deaths.

Now he was going to be a parent himself. That odd tightness started in his chest again. He'd come over to Rachel's apartment to acknowledge his responsibility to her and the baby, but now, seeing her so hurt and small, he realized his heart hadn't really been in it. He'd resigned himself to doing his duty toward her and their child—nothing else. Just his duty.

But now, someone had hurt her and could have hurt his baby—their baby. Something primal swelled up within him—a fierce protectiveness—adding to the mix of anger and that other emotion he couldn't name.

"Rach," he said, glancing over at her.

Her eyes met his.

"I swear to God, I'm going to find who did this. And until I do, I'm not letting you out of my sight. You and that baby are my responsibility, and I'll be damned if I let anyone get close enough to hurt you again."

Rachel's brow wrinkled and she looked down at the water glass.

He watched her trace the condensation on its side with a finger. She hadn't liked what she'd heard, and he knew why. His intention had been to reassure her, but it hadn't come out exactly right. He'd sounded harsh and angry.

From the look she'd given him, it appeared she didn't believe him. She had to know he could take care of her. So why did he get the feeling she didn't want him to?

THE POLICE AND the EMTs arrived at the same time. Rachel found herself in the hands of two young men in scrubs who cleaned the blood from her scalp wound, then called over a policeman who took photographs. Once he was done, one of the EMTs applied something to the cut that stole her breath, it stung so badly.

"I'm putting sterile strips on the cut," he told her. "It's not bad enough for stitches. It's shallow and about two centimeters—that's about three quarters of an inch."

She nodded.

"Don't wash your hair for a day or two, then have it looked at. It should be closing up by then. If your head hurts, take some acetaminophen or ibuprofen. And it would be a good idea if you stayed with someone tonight, so they could check on you about every four hours, just to be sure your pupils are equal in size and you aren't feeling dizzy or seeing double."

She didn't have anyone she could stay with, certainly no one she could call at this hour. But that was okay. She felt fine, except for the throbbing headache and the blurred feeling in her brain.

As she thanked the EMTs, she saw Detective Neil Chasen coming toward her. He was a big man, tall and muscular, with skin so dark it almost looked black. She smiled at him.

"Rachel, how's your head?"

She made a wry face. "Hurts."

"Yeah, I'm sure." Neil sat down at the kitchen table. "I'll get this over with as quickly as possible. I need to ask you some questions about the person who attacked you."

She nodded gingerly. Every movement of her head increased the throbbing. She much preferred the intense but quickly gone burning of the medication to the persistent headache she had now.

"Take me through what happened," Neil said. "Start with when you got home."

"I stopped at the grocery after work, so I got home about six. I put the groceries away, and decided to lie down for a few minutes." She paused, debating whether to tell Neil she was pregnant. She decided it wasn't relevant. "I don't think I went to sleep. I heard a crash, like wood splintering, then I heard the front door swing open and hit the wall. It squeaks. So I knew someone had broken in."

"Do you know what time that was?"

"No." She glanced at the kitchen clock. It read 7:15. "Maybe 6:15 or so?"

"Okay." Neil was scribbling in his notebook. "Go ahead."

"I grabbed my keys and ran for the back door, but before I could get there, he grabbed me from behind and hit me on the head."

"When you say grabbed—"

She closed her eyes, trying to relive the terrifying feeling of his hand stopping her. "I think he caught the back of my shirt."

"Where's the wound? Can I look at it?"

"Sure." She turned her head and pulled the hair away so he could see the cut.

"It's on the left side." Neil sat back down and wrote some more. "He must have grabbed you with his right hand and swung the weapon with his left." Neil acted out his theory. "Maybe a lefty. Then what?"

"I guess it stunned me. I fell. I remember hearing him throwing things around and cursing."

"Are you sure it was a man?"

She nodded. "I could tell by his voice, and—and after-shave or cologne. He smelled like a man."

"Good. Could you identify the aftershave?"

"No."

"Did he—touch you again, or talk to you?"

Rachel shuddered at the implications of Neil's words. "I was afraid to move. I wanted him to think I was still unconscious. He threw something—or kicked something, cursed loudly and slammed the front door." She took a breath. "I didn't know whether he'd left or not, so I still didn't move."

"Okay. When did you move?"

"I heard someone come in. I could hear their footsteps. Then I heard—I heard Ash's voice." Rachel's eyes filled with tears and she put her hand over her mouth to stifle a sob. "I'm sorry, Neil. I was just so scared. I thought the man had come back."

Neil nodded.

"But it was Ash—" She sniffed.

Neil dug in his pocket and handed her a neatly folded handkerchief. "Have you had a chance to look around? Is anything missing?"

She shook her head and handed back his handkerchief. "I haven't looked."

"Why don't we look now?"

Rachel let Neil take her hand and help her up. They went through the rooms. The man had trashed each one, but for all the disarray, Rachel couldn't tell that anything was missing. Not even her jewelry, which was scattered across the top of her dresser.

"What about papers, case files, anything to do with a case you're working on?"

"I don't bring anything home that has to do with a specific case," she muttered, grimacing at the stinging pain from the head wound.

"Nothing?" Neil asked. "Not even a laptop or PDA?"

She shook her head. "No. Nothing. We have to sign out case files. I've never signed one out. If I have to work late, I stay at the office."

"Does everyone know that? Is it possible that someone might break in here thinking you've got files at home?"

"I'm sure it's possible. You think that's why he broke in? Why he didn't steal anything? I thought he was just a burglar who probably didn't know anyone was home."

Rachel didn't want to think about the possibility that the intruder might have targeted her. She worked on sensitive cases, identified dangerous criminals. So she was very happy that her job was insulated from direct contact with criminals and victims.

She knew a lot about police procedure and handling dangerous situations from her dad. He'd taught her how to shoot and clean a gun. She even had a carry permit. Then her dad had been killed when he'd answered a call about a domestic dispute.

After he had died, Rachel, who'd almost let him talk her into going to the police academy despite her mother's opposition, went back to graduate school and got her Ph.D. in Molecular Biology.

"Could be."

"What?" Rachel blinked. She'd drifted off into thought. She pressed her fingers against the skin near the cut.

Neil was still talking. "I'll need a list of your current cases. Is there one that stands out? That might be particularly controversial?"

Rachel bit her lip. Of course there was. The Christmas Eve Murders. Could the man who had assaulted her have been looking for information about Rick Campbell's DNA? She glanced over at Ash, who was talking to one of the EMTs. She wasn't supposed to know whose DNA it was. And neither was Ash. She tried to corral her thoughts so she could answer Neil.

"I work a lot with cold cases, where DNA is analyzed or reanalyzed. Those files are usually sanitized." That was true, as far as it went. She hoped Neil would take the cue and request those official files rather than asking her anything else about them. She knew Neil would find the Christmas Eve Murders in with the rest of her recent cases, but she didn't want to call attention to it. Let him be the one to bring it up.

"Okay." Neil pocketed his notebook and stood. "I'm sure I'll have more questions later, but that's it for now." He smiled and shook her hand. "Have you got someplace to go? Need a ride anywhere?"

She shook her head as Ash came over to join them.

"Anything?" he asked Neil.

"Not much. Rachel can't identify anything that's missing. I think we're going to have to assume the break-in was connected with one of her cases until we can prove otherwise."

"One of her cases? Which one?" Ash glanced at her sidelong.

Neil shook his head. "I'm going to have to get a list of all her recent files—see what turns up."

Rachel saw Ash's shoulders visibly relax. He'd been worried she'd tell Neil about Campbell.

"How's your head?" Ash asked her.

Before she could answer, Neil spoke again.

"There is one more thing," he said.

Rachel looked at him.

"How did you happen to find her?" This was directed at Ash.

Rachel realized she hadn't even thought about why Ash had come to her rescue. She'd just been thankful that he was there.

Ash frowned at Neil, then shrugged. "I had something I needed to talk to her about. I got here a little after six, because I figured she'd be home from work by then."

"You missed her at work?"

Ash's lips thinned. "This wasn't work-related," he said shortly.

Chapter Five

It was nearly midnight before they made it back to Ash's house. The crime scene guys had cut Rachel a break and allowed her to pack a small bag.

A very small bag, she thought, looking at the change of underwear and the work outfit she'd grabbed. The pants and sweater were a dark chocolate brown. She hadn't remembered to get shoes, so she'd wear the black pumps she had on with the brown outfit.

Not only would she have the St. Louis police hovering over her, she'd have the fashion police on her tail. She giggled and then winced as the throbbing in her head increased.

She'd seen Ash's guest bedroom before. It was small and furnished with period pieces that she knew came from his aunt Angela's attic. As had the comforter—a flowered print with ruffled pillow shams.

Smiling, she turned back the comforter, expecting to find that the bed was bare, but no, it was made—with pink sheets. This had to be the work of his aunt.

A rap on the open door behind her made her jump.

"What's so funny?" Ash asked. He'd changed from his dress pants and shirt to jeans and a white T-shirt that gave her more than a hint of his rock-hard abs and left his biceps bare. He was holding two folded white towels that made his tanned skin shimmer in contrast.

Her fingers tingled with the remembered feel of his skin, and so did her body. "Funny?" she asked.

"I heard you laughing."

"Oh. The pink sheets and the floral comforter. I'm guessing you didn't pick them out yourself."

"Hmph," he muttered, and handed her the towels. "I don't think I have any pink towels."

"I actually prefer white. They look and feel so *clean.*"

"Right." Ash was obviously not enjoying this conversation about linens. "Need anything else?"

She shook her head.

He turned to leave, but she stopped him. "Ash?"

"Yeah?"

"Thank you for letting me stay here. I'm really sorry about—everything."

He shook his head, waving away her apology. "It'll only be for a few days. I can handle it if you can."

"Handle it?" she repeated. "Please don't let me put you out."

"I didn't mean it that way," he said, backing out of the door. She slammed it behind him, blinking. For some silly reason, his offhand comment had hurt her feelings.

I can handle it if you can. Like he was dreading having her here. No, not even that. It was more like he couldn't care less whether she was here or ten thousand miles away.

But she remembered the catch in his voice and the concern in his eyes as he'd asked her if the baby was all right. Had she imagined that he was terrified that the baby was hurt?

She rubbed her damp eyes. She was reacting to everything that had happened. That was all. That and her changing body. The doctor had warned her that the hormones that were surging through would make her not only tired, drowsy and queasy, but also highly emotional.

As she ran her palm across her gently rounded stomach, her eyes stung again. She set her jaw in determination. She had to get a grip. She was a scientist, and her job required analysis, not *feelings.* She couldn't afford to spend the next seven months fighting back tears.

Piling underwear and a camisole pajama set on top of the towels, she headed for the hall bath. Checking behind the mirror and behind the shower curtain, she discovered there were no toiletries. No soap. No shampoo. Not even toothpaste. She went into the kitchen and found Ash staring at the back of a frozen entrée.

"Do you have shampoo? Soap? Toothbrush and toothpaste?" she asked.

He looked up and frowned. "What?"

"I didn't bring shampoo or anything with me. Can I borrow yours?"

"You're not supposed to wash your hair."

"Soap and toothbrush then."

He seemed to be studying her, the frown still furrowing his brow. What was wrong with him? "Ash? Soap? Toothbrush?"

"Yeah." He looked back down at the frozen dinner in his hand. "In my bathroom," he said.

"Do you want me to cook that for you when I get out of the shower?"

"No." He opened the freezer and tossed the bag inside. Then he opened the refrigerator. "I've got stuff for sandwiches. You hungry?"

"Not really. Just exhausted." She cocked her head. "Are you all right?"

He let go of the refrigerator door. It drifted shut. "Sure. I'm fine. What about you? Is your head still hurting?"

"It's getting better. I'm going to take my shower now."

He nodded, but as she turned to go, he stopped her with a hand on her arm. "Are you sure you feel well enough to take a shower?"

She smiled quizzically. "Of course. I'm fine."

"I could—I could help you bathe if you don't feel like standing in the shower." He blushed.

"No!" she said quickly. "I mean, no, thank you. I promise you I'm fine."

"Okay," he said, but he didn't sound convinced.

Escaping before he changed his mind, she found a new bar of deodorant soap under the vanity in Ash's bathroom and a half-squeezed tube of toothpaste lying on the sink. Behind the mirror was a new toothbrush, the type the dentist hands out.

Heading back to the hall bath, she took a hot shower, taking care not to wet the cut on her head. Then she brushed her teeth and put on her pajamas. She eyed herself in the mirror, deciding that the pajamas weren't sexy or suggestive by any definition. They were pale blue and the drawstring bottoms had teddy bears on them.

Besides, Ash had seen her in less—much, much less. She watched her cheeks turn pink in the mirror. "A little late to be blushing now," she admonished herself, then yawned.

Folding the towels and gathering up her clothes, she left the bathroom and then stuck her head into the kitchen. Ash was still there, drinking orange juice from the carton.

The sight of him leaning against the counter twisted her heart as poignant memories flooded her brain. Memories of weekends spent making love, watching the Cardinals play, cooking together. Actually, she'd usually cooked while he teased her by sliding a cold beer bottle or soda can across the back of her neck or her arm or any of several other intimate places.

She shivered. How many times had they ruined dinner because he'd turned off the food and carried her into his bedroom? They'd made love for hours, then ordered pizza.

She gave herself a mental shake. That was then. And it was how she'd ended up pregnant, while Ashanova had smiled charmingly and moved on.

Poignant memories dissolved into bitter ones. "I'm done," she said. The words came out more harshly than she'd intended.

Ash turned and the carton stopped, halfway to his lips. If she didn't know better, she might think that green gaze was stripping her bare as it traveled down to her toes and back up. And did it linger on her tummy? Her hand moved automatically, but she managed to stop it before her fingers could spread protectively across the barely discernible bump.

Before two seconds had passed, Ash's hand moved again and he was taking a long swallow of juice. She might have dreamed anything else.

"I'm going to get some water and go to bed."

"Want some orange juice?" he asked, holding out the carton.

She shook her head and got a glass from the cabinet and filled it with water from the refrigerator dispenser, then headed for the guest room.

"Rach, leave the door open. I need to check on you every couple of hours."

"What? Why?"

"Concussion, remember? The EMT told me to wake you and check your eyes and get you to talk to me."

Rachel shook her head. "I don't have a concussion. The symptoms would already be showing. I just looked at myself in the mirror. There's nothing wrong with my pupils. They're perfectly even."

"Still—"

"Besides, he said four hours—not two."

Rachel bit her lip and fought the slight sting at the back of her eyes. She didn't want him to check on her. She didn't want him looking at her while she slept.

For four months she'd slept beside him, breathing in his warm, sleepy scent, feeling his hard body against hers, feeling cherished and safe, protected and loved. And trying to ignore the voices of the well-meaning women at the precinct. *His motto is love 'em and leave 'em—happy.*

What Ash was doing now, he was doing from a sense of duty, just as if he were back in the army and facing a horrible assignment. His face, his whole attitude, radiated resignation and determination. He was the father of her child and no matter how onerous the job was, he would handle it.

She'd rather be watched by a drill sergeant than by Ash in his new role as duty-bound sperm donor.

"Fine," she said, hurrying into the guest room and turning off the light. She got into bed and turned her back to the door. She sniffed as quietly as she could and dried her eyes on the pillow case. She was not going to let him see her cry.

Ash PICKED UP THE JUICE carton, but it was empty. He tossed it into the trash.

Then he paced. Or more accurately, he prowled. After a second trip from the kitchen to the living room and back again, he glanced at his watch. 2:00 a.m. Damn. He wasn't the least bit sleepy. Unlocking his front door, he slipped onto the porch. Aunt Angie had insisted on giving him an ancient yellow metal porch glider. At the time he'd tried to refuse, thinking it was the ugliest piece of furniture he'd ever seen.

But he'd discovered that when he had trouble sleeping, or if he had a tough case, he liked to sit out there. He'd oiled it, and the smooth, silent back-and-forth motion relaxed him. Sometimes he'd fall asleep, but even if he didn't, the night air would clear his head and help him think.

Maybe it would help him tonight. He sat and closed his eyes, listening to the sounds. His house was on a cul-de-sac, so he didn't get much traffic, but the interstate was within earshot.

Sometimes, he found the muffled traffic sounds distracting, even relaxing. But not tonight. Tonight—or rather this morning, he had so much on his mind that his thoughts were not only racing, they were bouncing crazily from one problem to another.

Ironically, all his current problems involved Rachel.

She'd surprised him earlier when she'd walked into the kitchen. He'd realized he'd been trying to wrap his brain around the idea of being a father.

Then he'd looked up and there she was, in funny little pajamas with teddy bears on the pants, glowingly beautiful, even with the dark circles of exhaustion under her eyes.

He wondered what she'd say if she knew that on the same day he heard about the petition to test Rick Campbell's DNA, he'd been seriously considering calling her.

It had been a crazy thought, but he'd made up his mind that it was the only way for him to move on. Because he was having trouble getting Rachel Stevens out of his mind. Was it because he'd sensed something? There were plenty of old wives' tales, ranging from expectant fathers who had sympathy morning sickness to those who reported feeling the baby kick inside their own bellies. Ash gave a quiet snort.

No. Rachel had stuck in his mind for no other reason than all the stuff she'd left at his house.

Still, there had only been a few times he'd even considered revisiting a previous relationship. Of course he'd never done it. He'd always been committed to keeping things light and casual.

A split-second flash of headlights caught his attention. He glanced at his watch—2:15 a.m. One of his neighbors was coming home late on a weeknight. Usually Ash was the only one who came in at all hours, if he was on a case.

When he looked up again, the headlights were gone. Idly, thankful for something to distract him, he tried to figure out which house up the street the car had stopped at.

Then he saw a faint glint of the streetlight on metal. He froze. Was that the same car? Holding his breath, he listened. Yes, he could hear the soft whir of the engine. Someone was creeping down the street with his lights off. A guilty husband, hoping not to wake his wife? Or more likely a guilty teen. *Good luck with your mom not meeting you at the door, kid,* he thought.

As he watched, the car slowly crept into the cul-de-sac. No. This was no guilty husband or child. Whoever was in that car was acting suspiciously.

He half closed his eyes. He didn't want anything, not even lights reflected by his pupils, to alert the driver that he was sitting here. He wished he had his weapon, and that he didn't have on a white T-shirt, but there was nothing he could do about either right now.

There was no moon, but the streetlights allowed him to see that the vehicle was an older subcompact, maybe a

Ford Focus, and it was red—not the best color for sneaking around.

It hugged the right side of the cul-de-sac all the way around and then came to a stop directly in front of Ash's house. He held his breath again. People's senses were a little like animals' in that if something doesn't move, oftentimes a person wouldn't notice it. Ash was banking on that, and the partial cover of the bushes between him and the street.

He couldn't tell anything about the driver. The streetlights weren't bright enough to illuminate the inside of the car. The driver sat there with the engine idling.

After about three minutes, another flash of headlights blinded Ash. A second vehicle had turned onto his normally quiet street. Its headlights stayed on as it circled the cul-de-sac, their beams never quite close enough to Ash to expose him. Although their glow licked at his feet.

The car turned into the driveway three houses down and opened the garage door, pulled forward, then closed it.

A clicking noise and a flash of light brought his attention back to the vehicle parked directly in front of his house. The man had opened the driver's side door—to get out? Ash stole a narrow glimpse inside the car before the interior light went out and another clicking sound told him the driver had thought better of getting out of the car.

The dome light hadn't helped Ash get a look at the driver's face, but it had revealed one thing. The man in the car was holding a large silver handgun upward in his right hand.

Had he been prepared to shoot Ash's neighbor if he'd walked over to investigate the dark, idling car?

Ash stayed put for several more minutes. Finally, the car slowly and carefully drove away. Squinting and resisting the urge to run into the street, Ash tried to see the license plate, but it was as beat-up and dirty as the vehicle, and the best he could do was maybe a five and maybe a one.

He sat there for five minutes after the car disappeared down the street, but nothing happened, so he got up and went inside.

He'd already known he wasn't going to get much sleep tonight, the second night in a row, because he had to check on Rachel every four hours or so. But he hadn't reckoned on a late-night visitor adding another worry to the crowd of them that was chasing around in his brain.

He grabbed a dimmable flashlight and quietly slipped through the door to the guest room, which Rachel had left ajar.

"Rachel," he whispered. "Rachel."

She stirred. "Ash? Are you coming to bed?" she asked, obviously mostly asleep. She thought they were still to-gether.

Her husky voice sent memories spreading through him like wildfire. That soft midnight whisper had always been an instantaneous turn-on for him. He shifted uncomfort-ably. *Still was.*

He smiled wryly as he sat down on the edge of the bed. "No, Rach, I just need to check your eyes."

"My eyes?" she muttered, then, "Oh. My eyes." She sat up, the dark, sexy voice gone. "You can turn on the light if you want to."

He shook his head. "I'm going to shine this light into your eyes. It's pretty dim, so hopefully it won't be uncom-fortable. Ready?" He turned the light's switch to the lowest setting.

She nodded, but when he proceeded, she squinted. "They look fine," he said.

"Told you I don't have a concussion," she replied as she slid back down in the bed. "G'night."

"Good night, Rach."

He sat there for a few moments, staring at her pretty, serene face. He realized he was thinking about what her baby girl would look like. *Their* baby girl. Or boy. A boy. They might be having a boy. His gaze drifted to her stomach, its shape obscured by the covers. He wanted to touch it, feel the roundness where his baby grew. He squeezed his eyes shut and shook his head. What was the matter with him? He'd never cared a thing about kids.

Rachel murmured something in her sleep, startling him out of his reverie.

Following an impulse he wasn't sure he understood or liked, he leaned down and pressed a light kiss to her forehead, then slipped out.

He went to his bedroom and flopped down on top of the covers. He glanced at his alarm clock, but he wasn't going to need it. It was less than four hours until he had to get up, and he had plenty to think about to fill the time.

Had the person in the car been checking on him or Rachel? Was he the same man who'd broken into her apartment and assaulted her? Whoever he was, he was armed. And from the way he'd held the gun, Ash could tell he wouldn't hesitate to use it.

Ash got up and retrieved his weapon from the locked desk drawer where he kept it. Until he figured out who was trying to harm Rachel—and why—he planned to be armed 24/7.

Chapter Six

"Dr. Stevens, this is Commissioner Washington's secretary. The commissioner needs to see you in his office immediately."

Rachel almost choked on a mouthful of decaffeinated coffee. She'd barely made it to her desk in time to catch the phone. She swallowed and cleared her throat. "Of course. I'll be right there."

She told Vanessa where she was going and rushed to her car, her mind racing with questions. What could the commissioner want to see her about? Her attack? The DNA report? The only times she'd been contacted by the police commissioner's office was when they'd wanted her to run a specific DNA sample.

When she arrived, the secretary escorted her right into his office, which was filled with high-ranking law enforcement officials.

"Dr. Stevens," Commissioner Washington said, acknowledging her without rising. "I believe you know everyone here—Deputy Chief Hammond, Lieutenant Colonel Barr, head of Criminal Investigations, Lieutenant Colonel Harris, my chief of staff, District Attorney Jesse Allen and A.D.A. Tim Meeks."

She nodded at each of them in turn. Tim smiled at her and winked. She looked away. Their paths rarely crossed, which was a good thing. After Ash had turned cool, she'd gone out with Tim a few times but when he had pushed her to have sex, she'd refused. He hadn't called her since, and that was fine with her.

"In about—" Washington looked at his watch "—ten minutes, we'll be holding a press conference to announce that convicted murderer Rick Campbell is, as of today, a free man, because of a DNA analysis you performed for me. We're just going over the particulars."

Oh, no. The commissioner was about to go public with the results of the DNA analysis. He was going to tell the press that Campbell was innocent of the Christmas Eve Murders.

Had anyone told Ash? She closed her eyes as her head started to throb.

"I want you available in case there are technical questions. Now—" the commissioner held up a hand "—I don't want too much technicality, so be succinct and keep it as close to a layman's level of understanding as possible."

"Yes, sir," she said, hearing the hollow ring in her voice. She should have taken the doctor's advice and called in sick today. But that would have meant being around Ash's house all day by herself, and she was sure he wouldn't like that.

Not that it mattered what he liked or didn't like. After he saw her standing on the podium with the commissioner, he'd never forgive her.

"All of you," the commissioner continued, "be aware that Rick Campbell and his family will be standing with us. I'll make the announcement, answer a few questions and call on you if necessary." His gaze settled on Rachel. "Then I'll turn the microphones over to the Campbells' lawyer."

He stood and adjusted his dress blues. "We will all

remain on the platform until the Campbells are done. Is that understood?"

The others stood as one, and Rachel followed their example. "Yes, sir," they said in unison.

As they walked out, Tim Meeks put a hand on Rachel's arm. "Pretty exciting, isn't it? I mean, to be the DNA expert who freed Campbell."

"It's gratifying to know that I helped to set things right."

"Yeah." Tim adjusted his tie and leaned in close to her ear, as if he were telling her a huge secret. "You know it was me, right? I pushed Jesse into accepting the Campbells' petition for DNA analysis."

"Really?" Rachel replied. So it *was* Tim, just like Ash had suspected. He'd certainly feel vindicated. "Why?"

"What?" Tim asked. "Why what?"

"Why did you do it? I mean, what made you choose *this* case?"

"Are you kidding? The *Christmas Eve Murders?* One of the most notorious and grisly murder cases in Missouri history. It was a win-win!"

As they walked toward the platform, where a podium had been set up, Rachel said, "Win-win? I don't understand."

"If the DNA was Campbell's, we'd be sending the message that we're open to reexamining a case if the situation warrants it. But if the DNA *wasn't* Campbell's—" Tim grinned "—we'd be freeing an innocent man and going after the real killer."

It did sound like, no matter what, that the D.A.'s office would come out smelling like a rose.

"And this was your idea?" she whispered as they began lining up on the platform behind the commissioner.

In front of them, the reporters crowded the platform, yelling questions while photographers snapped stills or operated video cameras. They reminded Rachel of piranha who'd sensed blood.

"Yes. Well, mine and Jesse's." Tim nodded in D.A. Jesse Allen's direction.

The commissioner held up his hands to quiet the reporters and began speaking. So Rachel stood up straight and composed her face. To her dismay, Tim leaned toward her again. "Want to grab lunch after this?"

She did her best to hold on to her pleasant expression. He was asking her out, right in front of a crowd of reporters? "No," she whispered and took a tiny sideways step toward Hammond.

Rachel stood on the platform between Tim and Chief Hammond, trying to pretend her head didn't hurt. She clutched the folder that the commissioner's chief of staff had handed her as they had left the office. He'd whispered that it was a copy of her report.

When she'd first gotten to the platform, she'd craned her neck to get a look at Rick Campbell. He was standing to the left of the commissioner and a short man holding a folded document—his lawyer. On his other side was a gray-haired woman and a man who looked to be in his late thirties. Looking at Campbell and at them, it was obvious they were his mother and brother.

Campbell himself was a small, thin, average-looking man with graying hair and a furtive way about him that Rachel had seen in others who'd been in prison. She shivered as his pale blue eyes met hers. He didn't look away, nor did he smile. He just nodded solemnly at her. Rachel turned her gaze to the commissioner, who had just finished his opening statement and was inviting questions.

The reporters fired questions like volleys of buckshot at Commissioner Washington. After he'd answered dozens of them about why this new DNA evidence had just come to light, how the St. Louis Metropolitan Police Department could defend such a heinous miscarriage of justice, and whose heads were going to roll to pay for the conviction and imprisonment of an innocent man, the question Rachel had been dreading finally came.

"Commissioner, just exactly how accurate is this new DNA evidence? How certain are you that Campbell is innocent and, if he didn't kill Joseph and Marie Kendall, who did?"

Rachel waited, not breathing, as the commissioner turned to her and nodded. He turned back to the microphones.

"This is Dr. Rachel Stevens. She is a senior criminalist in our crime scene unit. Her specialty is forensic DNA. She ran the sample. She can answer a few questions about her findings."

Rachel touched her hair to be sure her bandaged wound was covered as she stepped to the microphone. She'd carefully combed it this morning and secured it by a band at the nape of her neck.

Her brain was whirling with facts related to the DNA sample, but before she could speak, several reporters started shouting questions.

"Did you know whose sample you were analyzing?"

"How certain are you that Rick Campbell is innocent?"

"If the sample doesn't match Rick Campbell, who does it match?"

Rachel held up her hand in a useless gesture to stop the barrage. To her surprise, the crowd fell silent. She took a deep breath. "Forensic DNA today *is* an exact science. Only about one-tenth of one percent of the DNA in humans differs from one person to the next. We use these variables to generate a DNA profile of an individual. We can use blood, hair, saliva and other body tissues and products."

She took a breath, fully expecting to be interrupted with more questions, but her audience seemed rapt.

"The way forensic DNA analysis works involves obtaining samples from crime-scene evidence and from one or more suspects, extracting the DNA from each sample, and analyzing it for the presence of a set of specific loci or markers, as they're often called. If the sample profiles don't match, then that suspect did not contribute the DNA in that collected sample. If the patterns match, the suspect *may* have contributed the evidence sample."

Then the floodgates opened. Reporters fired questions so rapidly that all Rachel heard was a roar.

"Please," she said into the mike. "Please. I can't understand you. Let me continue."

Once again the reporters quieted down.

She opened the folder containing the report that the commissioner's chief of staff had handed her as she walked out of the office. When she looked down to refresh her memory of the exact percentages, she was surprised to see that it was an unsanitized copy of her report.

"This is information from the report I submitted to the commissioner related to the Christmas Eve Murders. My analysis of the sample resulted in a 99.9935 percent probability that the tissue, blood and hair samples, other than the family's, that was collected at the scene all belong to the same individual."

She looked up and through the sea of faces crowding the podium on the steps of the building where the commissioner's office was located. Her eyes met the dark, stormy gaze of the man who'd fathered her baby, and whose life she was destroying with this information.

I'm so sorry, Ash.

"When I compared these samples to the sample submitted by the person convicted of this crime, the result was a

0.0000003 percent match. That's six zeroes. A three-in-a-million chance that Rick Campbell is even related to the person who committed those murders."

As the cacophony of questions flared, Rachel pointed to a fresh-faced young man. "Yes?"

"Three in a million? What exactly does that mean?"

"As I said, it indicates that Rick Campbell and the person whose blood and tissue were found at the crime scene are not the same person. In fact, they're not even related."

"But there are at least two other people out there whose DNA matches Campbell's?"

Rachel shook her head. "No. This is why I referred to DNA profiling as an exact science. With the exception of identical twins, it is so rare to find two people whose DNA exactly matches, that I'm not aware of a single case." She took a long breath, prepared to explain the makeup of a single strand of DNA, but the commissioner stepped to the microphone.

"All right, that's enough. Rick Campbell and his family are here. We'll give them a chance to speak." He introduced their attorney.

Rachel hardly heard a word that was spoken for the next forty minutes, during which Campbell's lawyer, his parents and finally he took the microphone. All of them were bombarded with questions. Most of the questions revolved around how it felt to be a free man—or to have their son or brother free—after so many years.

She concentrated on staying upright. She was tired and nauseated, her head hurt and that swallow of coffee was the only thing in her stomach.

Finally Rick Campbell held up his hands and shook his head. His lawyer clasped a hand on his shoulder and took his place at the microphone.

"No more questions, please," the lawyer said. "Rick still has a lot of red tape to cut through before he can go home. And I'm sure he'd much rather be doing that than standing here talking to you." The lawyer turned away from the microphone.

Campbell waved, then glanced toward Rachel and nodded. It appeared that he was nodding thanks to the city officials, but his gaze held hers and never faltered. He was nodding at her. Then he turned and linked arms with his mother. They, his brother and his lawyer left the podium.

At the same time the commissioner stood straight, turned smartly on his heel and led the way for his entourage. They paraded back inside the building to the elevator. There he stopped.

"Dr. Stevens," he said, turning to offer her his hand. She shook it. "You did an excellent job out there. Handled the reporters nicely. Thank you."

He and the rest of the big shots got on the elevator. Tim stayed behind. "Come on," he said. "I'll give you a ride back."

"No, thank you," she said. "I drove."

"Then I'll walk you to your car."

"Tim." She sighed. "That is really not necessary. I'm parked right out there." She wished he'd stop being so persistent. She didn't want to say or do anything that might encourage him, but she didn't like being rude.

"Me, too," he said, grinning.

"Fine." She gave up and headed toward the parking lot with Tim beside her.

"Rachel, listen," he said as they walked. "I want to apologize for how I acted on our last date. I was wrong, and I do want to see you again."

Rachel spotted her car and, to her dismay, she saw Ash

pacing back and forth beside it. She stopped and faced Tim. "I am sorry, but things are—complicated right now," she said.

Tim's mouth curled in a wry smile as he looked at her, then at Ash. "Yeah. So I see." He turned on his heel and stalked away.

Rachel walked over to her driver's side door and clicked the automatic door lock. Ash's face was set and his eyes were still filled with storm clouds.

"So between you and *Timmy* and the commissioner, nobody thought to tell me about the press conference? I had to find out at the last second from Chief Hammond. Not to mention that my family was blindsided. I barely had time to call them before the damn thing started."

"I was wondering if anyone had thought to tell you."

"Hammond called me in right before he left for the commissioner's office."

Rachel shrugged. "Then you knew before I did. I was summoned to the commissioner's office, and when I got there, Uncle Charlie was already there."

That seemed to take the wind out of Ash's sails. "Well, somebody dropped the ball. Uncle Craig is going to have his lawyer call the commissioner. We should have been involved. As the family of the victims, we should have been kept apprised of everything that was going on with any petitions to have evidence reexamined."

"You don't have to convince me. I agree with you, Ash," Rachel said. "Completely. I can't say what I would have done if I'd known whose sample it was I was running, but I can tell you I'd have thought long and hard about it."

Ash's stiff shoulders relaxed a little. "That's something, I guess," he said grudgingly. Then he looked at her assessingly.

"So you and Timmy," he drawled.

"Ash, I already told you, I am not dating Tim."

"You two looked real close there on the platform, whispering back and forth. And just now, too."

"Right," she said, exasperated. "I was whispering *no*."

Ash's mouth turned up as he looked at his watch. "I have to go. Chief Hammond wants to talk to me. He said to get with him as soon as the press conference was over."

"Are they done with my apartment?" Rachel asked.

"No, not nearly."

"When am I going to be able to go home?"

"Forget about going home. So far, we haven't found anything that even begins to explain why he broke in or whether your attack was planned or if you just got in his way. I've got the crime scene unit going over the place with a microscope. Until they come up with something, as far as I'm concerned, you're still in danger. And that means you stay with me."

Ash had intended to spend the morning trying to find out something about the car that had sat outside his house the night before, but first he'd been hit with the information about the press conference and then, Chief Hammond had told him that he needed to see him as soon as the press conference was over. He was glad Hammond had called him in. He wanted to talk to the chief, too.

Ash knocked on Chief Hammond's open office door. He was on the phone. He gestured for Ash to come in and sit. "Hell, no!" he yelled at the receiver. "Do you think I care who's in the hospital?…He should have thought about that when he was taking all those long weekends….No, he's taking too much time off. One more hour this week and you suspend him, *without* pay. And by the way, when he gets in, send him back to canvass that neighborhood again on the Loyce case. From the way his report reads, he did a bad job the first time. He needs to cover *all* bases. I won't tolerate loose ends."

Ash winced. He was pretty sure he knew who Hammond was talking about. One of the uniformed officers in the district had a child with leukemia. Ash knew the police department was shorthanded and everybody needed to pull their weight. But Hammond had a reputation as a hard-nosed boss.

After a few more curses and orders, Hammond hung up. "Damn, I hate shoddy police work," he said with a shake of his head. Then he greeted Ash.

"Kendall, how are you and your family holding up?" he asked, his voice changing from hard to concerned.

"As well as can be expected, I guess. I wish I'd known about the news conference in time to warn my family."

"I know. I was under strict orders not to mention it to anyone. But I gotta tell you, I had a hard time keeping it to myself. I spent a lot of time with your aunt and uncle during that whole investigation. We got to be good friends."

"I remember," Ash said. "They've always been so grateful that it was you heading up the investigation. I'm grateful, too."

"Hey, it was my case. And you're no cop at all if you don't put your whole heart into every single case." Hammond shook his head. "You kids were so sad and scared. It 'bout ripped my heart out."

Ash glanced at the wall behind Chief Hammond. There were several distinguished service awards, one dated in March after the Christmas Eve Murders. Next to it hung a photograph of him being sworn in as the youngest deputy chief to ever head the Ninth Division of the St. Louis Metropolitan Police Department. The date on the photograph was less than five years after the murders. Judging by the wall, it was obvious that Hammond's career had been made by his role in bringing Campbell to justice for the Christmas Eve Murders.

Hammond followed his gaze. "That's right," he said as if reading Ash's mind. His chest visibly swelled with pride. "It was the Christmas Eve case that landed me the deputy chief position."

He paused and shook his head. "I never wanted to profit from your parents' deaths, but I like to think that in this position, I've been able to help other families whose lives have been touched by tragedy."

He turned back to Ash. "That probably sounds pompous. I don't mean it to. I think it's a great thing you've done, becoming a detective. You know what I'm talking about—being able to help other people."

Ash nodded, not quite sure what to make of Hammond waxing philosophical like this. He took the discussion back to Campbell. "I've read the case file and the newspaper accounts of the investigation. Was Campbell the only suspect?" he asked.

Hammond's demeanor changed, and he eyed Ash narrowly. "We nabbed him a few streets away. He had some rare coins and jewelry on him that he'd taken from a couple of your neighbors' homes," he said, ticking off the items on his fingers. "He was out on bail for some previous burglaries, plus he had scratches on his arms. The blood type was O positive, the same type blood as under your mother's fingernails. It was pretty much an open-and-shut case."

Ash nodded. He remembered all that from the case file. "And there was basically no DNA testing at that time, right?"

"That's right," Hammond said, scratching his neck as he settled again in his desk chair. "I don't think there was even a DNA lab in the States back then. If there was, it probably belonged to the FBI. Nope, we used every resource we had and every bit of evidence pointed to Campbell."

"It's so strange now, to think that it was someone else who actually killed them," Ash said.

"Listen to me, son." Hammond sat up straight. "If that DNA isn't bogus, then I'm a monkey's uncle."

Hammond was as vehement as Ash and his family had been that Campbell had to be the murderer. But no matter what any of them felt and thought, Ash was sure of one thing. "Rachel wouldn't falsify data," he said firmly.

"Aw, hell, that's not what I'm saying." Hammond picked up a pencil and jabbed the air with it. "All I'm saying is, what if somebody managed to switch the samples or something? 'Cause I'm telling you, Campbell was there. It had to be him. I always figured he went into your folks' bedroom by mistake and surprised them in their beds, then had to kill them." He rocked back in the desk chair, the spring squealing. "I'm going to look into that. I know what we saw and I know how Campbell acted. He's guilty as sin, and I'm not going to sleep until he's back behind bars where he belongs."

Hammond spread his hands. "That was all I wanted, son. Just to tell you that I'm on your side in all this. Come talk to me anytime."

"I have a request, sir."

Hammond frowned. "Sure. What is it?"

"I want to work the case."

"The case? Which—oh." Hammond stopped himself. "The Christmas Eve Murders? No. No way."

"I need to do this," Ash retorted. "Not for revenge, if that's what you think this is. My family and I need closure. I couldn't do anything back then. Now I can. Please."

Hammond shook his head. "Can't be done, son. The

commissioner has appointed a task force to reexamine all the evidence and follow up on any new leads."

"Then get me assigned to help them."

Hammond again shook his head. "Give it up, Kendall. The commissioner and the D.A. aren't going to let you within ten feet of that case."

Ash frowned in disgust. "I'd be an asset."

Hammond studied him. "You think you would, but trust me. When a case is this personal, when you've got this much riding on the outcome, it eats at you. You can't look at the suspects as innocent-until-proven-guilty, you get obsessive about dead-end leads—you keep trying to make the case fit the lead instead of the other way around." Hammond stared at Ash. "Nope. I've got to agree with the commissioner on this one."

"Well, they can't stop me from studying the case files," he said.

"You can't get to them. The task force has requisitioned every piece of paper in existence."

That's what they think. Ash clamped his jaw as he stood and held out his hand to Hammond. "Thank you, sir. I appreciate you talking to me and I understand what you're saying."

He turned to go but Hammond called after him. "By the way," he said.

Ash turned back. "Yes, sir?"

"You know Rachel's dad and me, we were big fishing buddies until he died on the job. Ned Stevens was one of the best."

"I'm sure he was," Ash said, unsure of where Hammond was going with this. Had he heard that Rachel was staying with him until her apartment was released as a crime scene? Was the chief about to warn him about Rachel?

Too late.

"He raised a mighty fine daughter, too. She was the apple of his eye, as they say. He even took her to the firing range with us from the time she was nine or ten years old. Taught her how to shoot his Glock 9 mm. Once she got her driver's license, he taught her how to tail a suspect without getting spotted."

Ash was surprised. "Rach—Rachel is proficient with a handgun?"

Hammond shrugged. "I don't know if she kept up the training after he died, but she was." Hammond waved a hand. "The reason I'm telling you this is Rachel's book smart, and she can handle herself, but she hasn't got much sense about men. You might want to watch out around her. She's been awfully chummy with A.D.A. Meeks lately. Did you know that he's the one that pushed the D.A. to get Campbell's case reopened? I think he smells a gold mine—careerwise."

"I heard the commissioner had the DNA redone." It still rankled Ash that Commissioner Washington hadn't given him the courtesy of a heads-up.

Hammond nodded. "That's right. But Meeks and Allen are the ones that put it before the commissioner. Hell, Meeks has been in here to question me two or three times already."

Ash knew Rachel had gone out with Meeks a couple of times, but he was pretty sure that was all. Despite the accusations he'd hurled at her in anger, he knew she wasn't seeing him. In fact, last weekend, he'd seen Tim Meeks with one of the legal secretaries from his office. Of course, that didn't mean that Meeks hadn't influenced Rachel.

He thought about his declaration to the chief. *Rachel wouldn't falsify data.* He was sure of that.

But what if the data she'd been given was tainted?

Chapter Seven

As soon as Ash left Chief Hammond's office, he headed for his desk. Anger boiled up within him at the commissioner and his damn task force. The argument that he couldn't work a case that he was connected to was ridiculous. If they'd give him a chance, he *could* be an asset. He could be rational about the case. Hell, he had twenty years' distance from that night. A niggling voice in the back of his mind said, *So why all the fury?*

Fury at injustice, at underhanded procedures and secret plans wasn't limited to those with a personal stake in cases, he argued with the voice, but his argument didn't hold much water, given the way he'd been treating people, especially Rachel.

Sighing, he turned his attention to the mysterious car from last night. All he'd been able to see of the license plate were two numbers, and he wasn't completely sure about them.

The plate could be from anywhere. He closed his eyes, trying to pinpoint the placement of the numbers he'd thought he'd seen. Damn it. Without knowing the state, it would be like finding a needle in a haystack.

He pulled up a page of current and prior Missouri tag styles on his computer. Then picturing the positions of the numbers he'd managed to make out on the vehicle's tag, he mentally overlaid them onto the computer screen. So, if the vehicle had a Missouri tag, the numbers should be in the third and fifth positions. He made out a request for a list of plates with those numbers in those positions and belonging to a Ford product. If that list didn't give him anything, he'd expand the search to nearby states. Like he figured, needle in a haystack.

Once he'd turned in the request, he decided to check on the trace evidence from Rachel's apartment. He picked up the phone, then set it back into its cradle. It would be quicker to run down to the lab, and he wanted to check on Rachel anyhow.

As he passed the DNA lab, he opened the door and peeked inside. Sure enough, Rachel was there. She was dressed in a white lab coat and sitting at one of the advanced scientific workstations, looking through the eyepiece of a big microscope, adjusting the focus with her left hand and writing with her right.

He didn't want to bother her. He'd acted on his protective urge, wanting to make sure she was all right. For a few seconds he stood there watching her. Her dark brown hair was slipping out of its hair band, exposing the small bandage on her head.

She was totally focused on the sample she was examining. She had no idea that he was there. It was the first time in a while that he'd had a chance to study her without her knowledge, and he took it.

She sat with her back straight in her crisply pressed white lab coat. She looked every inch the professional.

His gaze traced her profile. Her nose was short and tilted up at the end, making her look pixieish. He liked her nose, and her mouth, with its full lower lip. And her eyes, especially the odd reddish-brown ring around the golden irises.

She straightened and groaned softly. Her palm drifted to her belly and her mouth turned up slightly as she glanced down.

Ash backed away from the door, allowing it to close silently. For a few seconds he stood beside the door, eyes closed, savoring his mental picture of her smiling down at the child growing inside her. The sight had to be the most beautiful thing he'd ever seen.

His eyes stung and he swallowed against the lump that rose in his throat. He was *not* ready for any of this. Not being a father. Not being part of a newly created family. Hell, he wasn't even sure he was ready to be a grown-up.

He kept swallowing, but the lump wouldn't stay down. It tasted like fear, and he knew exactly what he was afraid of. After spending the last twenty years doing his best to harden his heart, what if it wouldn't soften even if he wanted it to?

He heard footsteps coming down the hall, so he straightened, wiped a hand down his face and headed toward the crime lab.

The CSI who'd been assigned to Rachel's case was taking close-up photos of a broken car windshield. "Detective, did someone call you?"

Ash shook his head. "Nope. About what?"

"Nothing. I mean, if you're down here to check on Dr. Stevens's case, I don't have any information for you."

"No information? Why not? I know you picked up viable samples."

"Yeah, we did. The intruder wore gloves, so there are no fingerprints. He did drop a couple of hairs. We put the information into CODIS, but didn't get a match."

"So the guy's not in the system," Ash said.

"Not in CODIS anyhow. If we had prints, we could check IAFIS to see if he has a record. But—" He shrugged.

"All right, thanks." Ash was disappointed. The FBI's Integrated Automated Fingerprint Identification System was invaluable to local law enforcement, *if* there were prints.

Frustrated, Ash checked his watch. He needed to get over to the courthouse, where he was scheduled to testify in a domestic violence case. On the way he called the uniformed officer who'd canvassed Rachel's building and parking lot.

"It's Kendall," Ash said when he reached the officer. "What did you find out on Rachel Stevens's case?"

"Not much," the officer told him. "I talked to the two people in the other apartments on her landing. The fourth unit's vacant. Both tenants were at work during the time of the break-in."

"How about the manager?"

"She wasn't much help. Apparently she drinks coffee, eats doughnuts and watches soaps all day."

"I want you to go back and talk to everyone again. See if you can find anyone who came in or out of the parking lot during that time."

"Again? Give me a break, Kendall. I've got other cases."

"Right. See if anyone saw a red Ford, a subcompact."

"Like a Focus?"

"Yeah. I could see two numbers on the plate. A five and a one. I've got a request in to run Missouri tags, but with only two numbers, I need a witness who saw the vehicle in Rachel's parking lot."

"Will do."

"Can you do it today?"

He heard a sigh through the phone line. "Yes, sir."

"Thanks."

WHEN ASH WENT BY THE DNA lab at five o'clock to see if Rachel was ready to go, she wasn't there. A lab assistant who was cleaning the biosafety hoods told him that she'd left early.

Ash hurried home, worried that she'd had another bout of nausea, but she wasn't at his house, either. He checked his phone but there were no messages. He called hers, but it went straight to voice mail.

He thought about going by her apartment, but he knew that her keys had been placed into evidence. So unless she had a spare key that she'd deliberately failed to turn over, she wouldn't be able to get in.

Looking at his choices—wait for her to get home or panic and put out a BOLO on her car—he decided, at least for the next two hours, to assume she'd gone shopping.

So he changed into jeans and a T-shirt and dug in the back of his closet for a file box that he'd stored there. He carried the box into the living room and set it on the coffee table. Then he opened the refrigerator's freezer compartment and stared inside at the contents. There was the frozen entrée he'd thought about making the other night, a half bag of French fries that looked like they were from the '90s and a gallon of ice cream. Slim pickings for dinner. He was just about to pull the frozen entrée out and read the back again when his phone rang.

It was his aunt. "Hi, Aunt Angie," he said. "How're you doing?"

"Oh, Ash, I need help with your uncle," Angie said, her voice shrill with anxiety.

"What's wrong? Is he okay?" Ash asked, closing the freezer.

"He's ranting and raving like a crazy man. He wants to dig out his old shotgun and shoot Campbell himself."

Ash suppressed a sigh. So Uncle Craig hadn't calmed down. "Have you called Devin?" he asked. Devin would have a better chance at talking their uncle down. He'd never been as close to Uncle Craig as Devin had.

"No," Angela said. "I thought you could come over here and tell him that you're going to arrest him if he doesn't stop threatening people."

"I can't arrest him for ranting and raving. Call Devin. He can talk some sense into him. I'm sort of tied up on an undercover assignment right now and I can't leave."

"How can the police do this?" Angela wailed. "How can they just one day say, *'Oh, well. We got the wrong guy. Sorry for the inconvenience.'*"

"I don't know. That's what I'm trying to find out."

"Well, please hurry. I'm not sure what's going to happen if someone doesn't stop Craig. And I don't think Natalie is sleeping."

"I've talked to Natalie. I think she's doing pretty well. Call Devin if you need someone tonight. I'll get over there to talk to Uncle Craig soon."

"All right," Angela said, but Ash could tell from her voice that she felt like he was giving her the brush-off. "Goodbye, dear."

As Ash hung up, feeling guilty, the front door opened and Rachel came in, carrying a leather satchel. When she set it down on the kitchen table, Ash heard a distinctive thump, the muffled sound of a heavy piece of metal against wood.

"What's that?" he asked.

Rachel took off her jacket and tossed it onto a nearby chair. "That's my weapon and ammunition."

She said it so matter-of-factly that Ash was taken aback. If Hammond hadn't given him a heads-up, his jaw would have probably hit the floor.

"Your weapon?" he echoed.

"Yes. It's been several months since I've gone to the range, so I went after work."

"Where do you keep it? Was it in the apartment when you were attacked?"

"No. I keep it in my car. I have a carry permit, but I keep the gun and ammo in the trunk."

"SLMPD doesn't require criminalists to carry a weapon," he said. "Why do you have a carry permit?"

She shrugged. "Dad thought it was a good idea."

"Let me see the gun."

She pulled a paddle holster from the satchel, slid the gun out and handed it to Ash, handle first.

Initially he checked to see if it was loaded. It wasn't. He inspected it, broke it down and reassembled it, then handed it back to her. He was impressed with its condition.

"Nice. When did you get it?" he asked, thinking he probably already knew the answer.

"It was my dad's. When he was killed on the job, the chief gave me his service revolver."

"This is the gun you learned to shoot with?"

She nodded, smiling wistfully.

"What else did your dad teach you?"

"I know how to flip a man who's rushing me. I can tail you without you knowing. And I can shoot a rifle, too, although I don't own one."

"You can't tail me."

"Bet I can."

Ash narrowed his gaze. "How come you didn't tell me any of this when we were dating?"

She shrugged. "I guess it never came up," she said, taking the gun back, checking the barrel. She reached into the satchel and pulled out a chamois cloth and wiped it down, then inserted it into the paddle holster and slid it back into the satchel.

"I've got to say, you look awfully sexy handling that gun."

Rachel's eyes widened. "Thanks, I think."

"What are you going to do with it?"

"Don't worry," she told him. "I'm going to clean it this evening and put it back in my car."

"It won't do you much good in the trunk," he said.

"That's what I was thinking. I'll probably keep it in the console, along with my carry permit," she said, stifling a yawn. She took the satchel into the guest bedroom, calling out, "I'm going to shower and then take a nap. Wake me if I sleep too long."

Ash stared across the hallway at the bedroom door for a second. She had always fascinated him with her contradictions. She was really sweet, but she could be stubborn as a mule when she made up her mind about something. She wore that geeky lab coat and almost always put her hair in a ponytail or a little knot at work, but when she let it down, literally and figuratively—she was irresistibly sexy.

And now, although her petite five-foot-three-inch frame appeared vulnerable and delicate, she owned and carried a Glock 9 mm semiautomatic pistol, a formidable handgun that served men twice her weight well.

And he'd told the truth when he'd said that watching her handle the gun was a turn-on. But somehow, it bothered him to see her with it and hear her talking about flipping or tailing men who could be dangerous. He remembered the image of her cradling the baby and smiling. Now, that was sexy. The idea that she was pregnant with a baby that the two of them had made was at once sexy, sweet, terrifying and humbling.

This was new territory for him. He'd had lots of fun with quite a few willing women, always taking precautions to keep them safe and stay safe himself. But up until Rachel, he'd never wished for a second chance with any of them. Nor had he ever once considered the idea of being a father.

He probably should have thought twice about letting Rachel stay here, but she could still be in danger and there was no one he trusted to keep her safe. No one but himself.

Ash looked at the box on his coffee table and reminded himself that he had plenty to do. Even if he couldn't be part of the official task force to find the real Christmas Eve murderer, he could form his own—a task force of one—to track down the man who had killed his parents.

Chapter Eight

Rachel woke with the delicious smell of cheese and garlic filling her nostrils. Her stomach rumbled as she slid her feet into pink house slippers. She was about to make a beeline for the kitchen when her phone rang. She glanced at the display. It was her mother.

"Hi, Mom," she said, sitting down on the bed.

"Don't *Hi, Mom* me. Why didn't you tell me that you were going to be on television? I had to find out from my neighbor. That was embarrassing."

Rachel rubbed her temple. "I didn't know until about ten minutes before. The commissioner called me just in time to get to his office before we had to be at the microphones."

"And that's not all. When were you going to tell me you were attacked?"

"Attacked? You mean when my apartment was broken into? I was going to call you on the weekend. How did you—?"

"I was talking to Charles Hammond's daughter."

Uncle Charlie's daughter. Of course. "It was nothing, Mom."

"Not from what I heard. I heard you got stitches."

"No. The EMTs just put strip bandages on the cut. It's tiny." Rachel's fingers explored the skin around the cut absently as she talked.

"Is there anything else I should know about?" her mom asked archly.

The words sent a jolt of apprehension through Rachel's chest. "No—" she said tentatively, then more strongly. "No. Why?" She couldn't possibly have heard that Rachel was pregnant. Nobody knew—except Ash.

"It just seems like I'm the last to know about everything lately. When are you coming over?"

"I'm not sure. I'm in the middle of this investigation right now. I was going to come maybe next weekend. How's that?"

"That would be great," Mom said. "We can start making plans for the holidays."

"I'll see you then, okay?"

"Okay, sweetheart. I'll make you some brownies."

By the time Rachel hung up, her stomach was demanding food. She headed for the kitchen, where Ash was stirring a pot on the stove—the source of the luscious cheese and garlic smell, and drinking a beer. He glanced her way, then did a double take.

She almost faltered. She looked down, wondering what he'd seen. Her top was sleeveless, but it had a fairly modest neck, and the bottoms were capri length.

"Want some sparkling grape juice?" he asked. "The bottle's open in the refrigerator."

"Great. That sounds good. What is that you're cooking?"

He shrugged. "Some packaged dinner. There's the package."

Rachel poured herself a glass of white grape juice and as she sipped, she read the ingredients. "Mushroom and spinach ravioli in a parmesan cream sauce. Yum. Have you got any more parmesan cheese?"

"Look in the cabinet," Ash said. "Doesn't the package say twenty minutes? Because I think it's done."

He took the pot off the stove and dished up two servings. He set the plates on the kitchen table. "I don't have any bread or stuff for a salad," he said apologetically.

"That's okay," Rachel replied. She saw the parmesan cheese on a high shelf, but she couldn't reach it. "Ash? Bring your long, lanky body over here and get the cheese for me. This is the most inconvenient thing about living with a six-foot-three-inch-tall man—" She stopped. Partly because of what she'd said, but mostly because he was behind her, reaching up. He was much taller than she, and his reach was ridiculously high. He grabbed the cheese and set it on the counter, but he didn't move away.

And Rachel needed him to, desperately, because having him pressed up against her back and butt was causing silly, fluttery feelings inside her. Feelings that had gotten her in trouble, in more ways than one. She'd spent many nights crying, knowing that to Ash, she was just another good time. Fun while it lasted, but definitely not forever.

She tried to move away, but he took her by the shoulders and turned her around, then put a finger under her chin. He was so close to her that she had to strain her neck to meet his gaze.

"Ash—?" she started, but he stopped her.

"Shh," he said. "I never wanted to hurt you."

"I know," she whispered. But he had anyway. And now he was standing too close. She could feel his rock-hard abs, shoulders and arms pressed into her. But there was something else rock-hard against her, too. He was aroused, and getting harder by the second. He slid his thumb across her lower lip and bent his head.

A deep, sharp arrow of desire shot through her, along

with a pointed dart of fear. If he tried to make love to her, right here and now, she wasn't sure she could refuse.

She sighed raggedly and pushed against his chest. But instead of stepping away, he brushed his lips across hers. "Don't cringe away from me, Rach. I can't stand that." He took a deep breath. "I want to be there for our baby," he said, his lips moving against hers.

What was he doing? Trying to co-opt her by taking advantage of her attraction to him? But for what? She felt her desire dissolve in a pool of fear that he would say anything to get what he wanted at the moment, which was her in his bed. Her hands against his chest doubled into fists.

"*Be there for our baby.* What does that mean exactly, Ash? Because it's hard to picture *Ashanova* play Daddy. Are we talking about every other Saturday, if you haven't been up all night—" She stopped herself before she said *screwing.*

He straightened and gazed down at her, an odd expression in his eyes. "We'd better eat." He stepped away and took the jar of parmesan cheese to the table.

Rachel sat, too. For a couple of minutes they ate in silence. "This is really good," she said finally.

"A gourmet meal in a bag," he responded drily.

She stared down at her plate, pushing the ravioli around. "What's happening with my apartment? Nobody's told me anything."

"Last I heard, CSI wasn't finished with it. Once they're done, the door will have to be repaired," he said.

"So when can I go back home?" she asked, exasperated.

Ash raised his gaze to hers. "You're in that big a hurry? Because I don't think you should return until we catch the guy."

"So you expect me to stay here?" she snapped.

"That was my plan. Look, Rach, I'm sorry about—" he gestured toward the counter "—that. I was out of line. I can guarantee you it won't happen again. I promise, you can feel perfectly safe here."

Rachel knew she'd reacted badly. She'd been sarcastic—maybe even mean. But she couldn't handle being this close to him. Not now.

Before, when it was all in good fun, she'd given as good as she'd gotten, until she'd fallen in love. Now she was carrying his baby. She didn't want to be reminded how charming and carefree he was, or how much she longed for his strong arms around her and his firm lips on hers.

She picked up her plate. "I'm tired. I think I'll go to bed early, as soon as I wash the dishes."

"Leave them," he said. "I'll get them. You can do them next time."

"Okay, you talked me into it." She got up and went to the refrigerator to pour herself another glass of juice. "I'll see you in the morning, then."

She closed the bedroom door and set the glass down on the bedside table. There were a few magazines on the lower shelf and she rifled through them. *Sports Illustrated. TV Guide.* Then underneath several copies of *Field & Stream* and some more of *TV Guide,* she found a couple of *Better Homes and Gardens.* "Thank you, Aunt Angela," she whispered and chose one.

But after a few minutes, she had to admit that the magazine couldn't distract her. Her thoughts were racing. She turned out the light and tried to concentrate on thinking about nothing. But Ash's handsome face, his warm, sexy body, the hard length of his erection pressing against her, swirled through her mind.

"Damn you, Ash," she whispered. "Why won't you leave me alone so I can get over you—again?"

ASH WAS SITTING ON HIS couch with manila folders spread out around him. His gaze traveled from one handwritten label to the next—Medical Examiner's Report, Crime Scene Photos, Fingerprints, Detective Reports, Witness Transcripts.

His hand hovered over the folder that held the crime scene photographs, but he couldn't make himself open it. He'd only seen them once, and once was more than enough. Besides, he didn't need photographs to remind him of the carnage in his parents' bedroom that Christmas morning twenty years ago. It was burned into his mind as if with a laser.

His dad, eyes wide and milky and a pool of blood congealing on his pajama shirt and the sheets. And his mother, with garish red splotches on her neck, her face swollen and blue and her left ring finger bloody and torn.

Ash closed his eyes against the memory, but it didn't help, so he rubbed them with his fingertips. It didn't erase the awful vision but it did stop the stinging and wipe away the dampness.

"Ash? Are you all right?"

He looked up, startled. Rachel was standing in the doorway. He had to blink to clear his vision. She was dressed in the blue pajamas with the teddy bears on the pants. Her hair fell in lazy waves around her face.

"Yeah," he said, sitting up straight. "Yeah. What are you doing up?"

"I don't know," she said, sitting on the other end of the couch with her feet under her. "I went to sleep, but something woke me. I think I was dreaming. My sleeping habits are all mixed up. It seems as if I can sleep anywhere and anytime except at bedtime in bed."

Ash half turned toward her, hoping in vain that she wouldn't notice the box and the folders. "Was it a nightmare?" he asked, pushing back a strand of hair off her shoulder.

"No. I can't remember. What are you doing? What are all those folders?"

"Nothing," he said, grimacing inwardly. "You ought to go back to bed. There's some aspirin in my medicine cabinet if you need some."

But Rachel picked up the folder nearest her on the coffee table. "This is a Medical Examiner's report."

He reached out to take it from her but she avoided his grasp and stood. She opened the folder. "It's your parents' case."

He blew out an exasperated breath. "*Now* you can recognize the case."

"Don't be an ass," she retorted. "It's written right here at the top of the form. What are you doing with this? I know you aren't authorized."

He shrugged. "I made copies."

"When? Not in the past two days."

"No." He stood. "I need some water. Want some?" he asked.

"Yes, thanks."

He filled two glasses with cold water and took one to her.

"How did you get these copies, Ash?"

"I've been a detective for four years," he said pointedly.

Rachel stared at him. "You've been copying documents from the case file all that time? Is that legal?"

He flopped down on the couch and took a long swallow of water. The chill spread through him, soothing the burning in his gut and head. "They're my parents."

She nodded and her eyes dropped to the open folder. For several seconds, she read in silence. She turned a page and read some more, then turned another page.

"Wait a minute," she muttered and flipped back to the first page. Then raised her gaze to his. "Your dad was shot, but your mother was strangled?"

"I thought you were going back to bed," he remarked.

"I'll go to bed when you do," she said, then blushed. She cleared her throat and continued. "You're obviously planning to go through all this, and I don't think you should do it alone."

"I'm fine," he said, grabbing the Fingerprints folder.

"Right. Now let me read what the M.E. says about the cause of death."

Ash opened the folder and let his eyes roam over the information that he already knew by heart.

After a few minutes, Rachel looked up. "Why would he shoot your dad but strangle your mother?"

Ash closed his folder, marking his place with a finger. He leaned his head back against the couch cushion and closed his eyes. "I don't know. Maybe he wanted to strangle both of them but Dad woke up so he had to shoot him."

"That doesn't make sense," Rachel said. "Plus he shot him at point-blank range. The M.E. notes that the bullet went all the way through your Dad's heart and the mattress and was embedded in the hardwood floor."

Ash grimaced. It irritated him that he was still bothered by all this. He'd read these reports several times over the past four years. He was a homicide detective. By now he should be able to look at this case with the same detachment he brought to his other cases. "What other explanation is there? Did he shoot Dad, then decide the gun made too much noise?"

"Maybe," she said. "Although, it wouldn't have made much noise pressed up against his chest like that."

Ash felt a shudder tighten his shoulders.

"I'm sorry, Ash. I'm not trying to be insensitive—"

"I know you're not. Go ahead. I've read all these findings over and over again, but I've never been able to talk about them to anyone, certainly not a criminalist. I'm glad you're going through the files with me."

She went back to the M.E.'s report. "The M.E. concludes that your dad was killed first, then your mom, because the blood spatter on your mom's face and neck was smeared. That makes sense. He says that it appears she tried to get out of bed, but was dragged back. Her feet were out from under the covers."

Ash closed his eyes. "That's right. I remember from the crime scene photos."

"You've got the crime scene photos?" Rachel said, her voice rising in excitement. "Let me see them."

He pointed toward the folder, then stood. "If you don't mind, I'll pass on looking at them again."

Rachel took the folder and stood. "I'll look at them at the kitchen table," she said, her voice suddenly soft and gentle.

He nodded and sat back down and read the fingerprint report again.

By the time Rachel had finished going over the photos, Ash had set the fingerprint report aside and picked up the folder containing the detectives' reports. He was deep into Hammond's record of his initial findings when Rachel came back into the living room and set the closed folder on the coffee table.

Ash looked up, his eyebrows raised and a lump of dread in his chest.

"Everything I saw was consistent with the M.E.'s report. I agree with his findings, just exactly as he wrote them. I don't think there's any need to review the photos again."

The lump in Ash's chest shrunk a little.

"But, Ash. There are a couple of things I don't understand."

"Just two?" he asked.

She shrugged with a wry smile. "Two in particular. First, according to the M.E.'s report, the abrasions on your mom's finger were made by ripping off a ring. But your dad wore a ring, too, and there was a gold money clip with several hundred dollars in it on the dresser."

Ash nodded. "The clip had Dad's initials on it. He might have figured it would be hard to fence."

"He could have left the clip. The money, though—why didn't he take the money?"

"Maybe he heard something when he was taking Mom's ring. Decided he'd better get out of there."

Rachel shook her head. "Maybe. But I'll bet your mom's ring was also engraved. It would make it hard to fence."

"I don't know whether it was or not. We could ask Aunt Angie."

"It's almost as if he shot your dad just to get him out of the way. Like his real target was your mom."

"That doesn't even make sense," Ash protested.

"I know it doesn't," she said. "It just doesn't feel like a burglary gone bad." She tapped the detectives' reports in Ash's hand. "The ring wasn't found on Campbell, right?"

"Yeah. Hammond notes here that Campbell must have dropped it. CSI searched around the grounds and turned his house upside down, but they never found it."

"Well, that wasn't the only thing he dropped, then. What happened to the gun?"

Ash frowned at her. "I don't know."

"Campbell didn't have a gun on him when they picked him up, right?"

"Right. And as far as I remember, they didn't find anything at his house."

"Right. Not even evidence of other burglaries. Just the jewelry and coins he had on him from the neighbors' houses."

Ash tapped the folder he was holding. "This is Hammond's initial report. It's—" he shook his head "—odd."

"Odd?"

"This morning after the press conference, he told me the case against Campbell was essentially open-and-shut. But according to his report, it's not. I mean, he lists all this stuff—the missing gun, Dad's ring and money clip, which were left untouched, the lack of fingerprints— but he doesn't say a word about the inconsistencies. The more I read, the more I find that doesn't add up. There's an awful lot that's not explained."

"I know. Are we missing something?" Rachel asked.

"I can't think what. But we're looking at the evidence twenty years later. Maybe we're jaded. We take all this technology for granted. I'm going to ask Hammond about it tomorrow."

"I'm sure Uncle Charlie did the best he could. My dad thought he was the best detective on the force."

"I'm not saying he did anything wrong. I just want to find out what I'm missing. What made the case open-and-shut."

"They should have had pretty good ballistics data. Where's the ballistics report?" she asked.

He pointed to the box. "In there somewhere."

She dug into the box and he went back to reading Hammond's report. After a few seconds, she pulled out a folder and sat down to read.

"Here it is," she said. "The forensics lab concluded that the bullet recovered from the floor underneath the bed came from a .22 caliber semiautomatic handgun. It says here that 'although the bullet was deformed from impact, the striations were consistent with a Smith & Wesson 22A.'"

She turned a page and then another. "They didn't find a match in the database, so the gun was clean."

"Yeah, at least it hadn't been used in a crime in this area. That's another thing about the technology. These days we can check if a gun's got a dead body connected to it anywhere in the country—hell, in the world."

Rachel nodded and read a little farther. "Campbell didn't have gunshot residue on his person or his clothes, either." She sat back with a long sigh.

"Hey. There's a page here where Hammond listed the suspects," Ash said. "He's got Uncle Craig listed here. Come on, Chief, that's just stupid. They weren't even living in Missouri at the time."

"Well, obviously they didn't pursue him for long," Rachel commented. "Who else?"

"Martin Thames. He was a senior vice president at Kendall Communications. Apparently he and my dad didn't get along at all, according to people Hammond interviewed. He's got a note here about recent firings at the company. There are four names here. All of them had alibis." Ash looked up at Rachel. "That's no surprise," he said.

"Right," she replied. "It was Christmas Eve."

Ash went back to reading. "Here he's got some jotted impressions. *Campbell—guilty?? Others—alibis. Jewelry & coins on Campbell's person. Nothing at house.*"

"Sounds like he had a pretty good circumstantial case against Campbell," Rachel said.

"Whoa," Ash said, surprised by the next few lines. "I'll be damned."

"What?" Rachel said, looking up.

"Listen to this," Ash said. "*Campbell claims saw man*

near Kendall house. Man saw him & ran. No description. No time. C. trying to throw off suspicion? I never heard this. There was someone else sneaking around the mansion that night."

Chapter Nine

Ash stared at Hammond's report. "I can't believe we were never told that another unknown suspect was there that night."

"Uncle Charlie doesn't say anything else about him?" Rachel asked.

"Not here."

"Ask him about it."

"I plan to," Ash said, flipping pages. "Here's the transcript of Devin's 9–1–1 call."

"Devin called?"

"Yeah. I remember hearing Natalie screaming—" Ash stopped. He had to swallow before he could continue.

Rachel scooted closer to him and laid her hand on top of his. It bothered him that her touch helped.

"I wondered why Mom was letting her cry like that. Then I heard Devin running down the hall. After a few seconds he screamed, too." Ash squeezed his eyes shut and rubbed them. "I ran and Thad was right behind me. By the time I got there and saw—what had happened, Devin was calling 9–1–1."

Rachel's fingers curved around his and she squeezed. "I'm so sorry, Ash." Her eyes were filled with tears.

He shook his head without opening his eyes. "I guess

it's never going to get easier," he said, his voice shaky. He took a deep breath.

"I hate to hear that but I understand. It's only been seven years since my dad was killed, but I still miss him so much." She sighed. "Anyway, you were saying Devin called 9–1–1."

"Right. The police came within a few minutes. There were two policewomen who took us back into the other wing, where our bedrooms were. Marie, the housekeeper, was there by then. She lived in the guesthouse. She held Natalie and rocked her, trying to calm her down."

He leaned his head back against the couch cushion again. "Somebody gave Natalie something to relax her and stop her from crying. Now that I think about it, it was probably the M.E. She went to sleep finally, and Devin and Thad and I all sat on Devin's bed. I have no recollection of what we did. But we were still there huddled together when Uncle Craig and Aunt Angie arrived late that evening."

"Ash—"

He held up a hand. "Don't, Rachel. I know."

"But—"

"Let's just talk about the case, okay?"

She nodded reluctantly. "Where were your aunt and uncle? Where did they come from?"

"They lived in California." Ash leaned forward with his elbows on his knees and his hands clasped. "They moved out there after my cousin Connor was killed when a car lost control and hit him on a sidewalk. But they came back here and took care of us. We were lucky to have them."

Rachel touched his hand again, but he pulled away and sat back. He didn't want her sympathy. He didn't much want her there at all while he dug through the piles of evidence about his parents' murder. But he valued her insight as a criminalist. And it was good to be able to talk about the case with someone. Nobody in his family could stand to listen to the details.

He picked up the Fingerprints folder, determined to get back to the facts. "The fingerprints are pretty straightforward. After ours were eliminated from the bedroom, there were no unidentified prints."

"None?" Rachel asked.

Ash smiled. "Marie was obsessive about cleaning. She and the day maid both wore gloves for everything—and I mean everything. She even wore gloves when she set the table."

"Wow," Rachel said. "What about the rest of the house?"

He nodded. "The glass in the front door was broken. But whoever did it was wearing gloves, because where prints should have been, there were only smears. Not even a partial."

"Whoever he was, he was certainly prepared. It sounds like he thought of everything."

"Too bad they didn't have DNA testing back then. They might have found a trace somewhere and been able to identify him."

Beside him, Rachel stiffened. "Oh, God," she gasped. "Oh, no!" Her hands flew to cover her mouth.

"What?" Ash demanded. "Are you sick?"

"No! No." She shook her head. "I just remembered something—oh, no." She tapped her forehead with her fist. "I am so stupid."

"Rach—"

She met his gaze, shaking her head. "The day I took the DNA report by the commissioner's office, I was on my way to a doctor's appointment." Her face was turning pale. "That was the day I found out I was pregnant."

Ash waited without speaking for her to continue.

"I had the office copy with me. I was going to take it

in the next morning and file it, but I forgot." She paused, pressing her lips tightly together.

"Ash, I was wrong when I told you that nothing was missing from my apartment. Whoever broke in took the DNA report that proves Rick Campbell is innocent."

"You're sure it was there?"

"Yes. I remember now. It must have fallen under the bed. I remember laying it on the bedside table that evening when I got home from work."

"The commissioner's office had the original, right?"

"Yes. But Ash, if the burglar knew I had that report, and broke in to get it—"

"Then the break-in is somehow connected to my parents' murder." Ash sat up. "I've got to call Neil and let him know."

RACHEL WAS WRAPPED IN Ash's strong arms. She came awake slowly, sighing with contentment. Her hand rested on his lean abs, which rose and fell with his slow, deep breaths.

She opened her eyes to darkness, the only light coming from the kitchen. Her head was nestled into the hollow of his shoulder. She took a deep breath, filled with the scent of him. He smelled like rain and fresh breezes—the scent of the detergent he washed his T-shirts in—and warm tan skin. She loved it.

She craned her neck slightly and looked up at his face. It was planed in shadows that cut across the strong line of his jaw. His eyelashes were ridiculously thick. They rested on his high cheekbones and cast feathery shadows on his skin. His nose was long. Its straight lines gave his face an elegant symmetry. By anyone's standards he was handsome. By hers, he was gorgeous.

His lashes fluttered as he opened his eyes. The kitchen

light reflected like green fire in his eyes as a corner of his mouth turned up. "Hi, there," he whispered.

"Hi, yourself," she answered.

"How'd we end up like this?" he asked, yawning.

She hadn't been awake long enough to think about that. She'd been basking in the feel of him. She laughed softly. "The last thing I remember was reading the detectives' reports."

Ash shifted. "That's right. I'd given you half of them." He yawned again and stretched.

"Well, someone turned off the lamp."

He closed his eyes and pulled her closer. "Oh, yeah. I did."

"Oh, yeah, you did?" she teased, sliding her hand around to his ribs and digging her fingers in.

"Hey!" he gasped, twisting away. "Stop it. I'm not ticklish."

"Oh, of course you aren't. You're just laughing to be polite."

He caught her hand. "Seriously, stop it. I don't want to wake up yet."

"No?"

He brought her hand to his mouth and kissed it. "No," he murmured, sliding her hand up to the back of his neck. "I like this dream."

"Mmm, me, too," she murmured, letting her fingertips drift across his nape.

His palm played along her forearm and on past her shoulder and down her rib cage. Her skin tingled where he touched. She traced the line of his jaw, thinking as she had when they were dating, that it was the barometer of his mood. Sometimes he clenched it so tightly the muscle quivered. Right now it was smooth and relaxed under his morning stubble. Absently, she twirled her finger in little circles on his skin.

She felt the muscles move as he smiled. "What are you doing?" he whispered.

"Giving you a jaw massage. It's where you keep all your tension."

"It's not tense now, is it?"

"No." Without thinking about what she was doing, she let her fingers drift to the corner of his mouth and around to touch his lips.

He shifted and wrapped his hands around her waist, pulling her on top of him.

"Ash—" she gasped. "What are you doing?"

But by the time she'd gotten the words out, he'd lifted her. She grabbed his forearms and straddled him, because that was the only place she could put her legs.

She opened her mouth to protest again, but his hands were sliding up, up, underneath her pajama top, until his thumbs caressed the underside of her breasts. His touch stole her breath and sent sudden hot longing searing through her. His erection grew rigid and tight through his jeans.

"Ash—" she rasped, trying and failing to sound like none of this was getting to her. "This is probably not a good idea—"

Her words were sucked right out of her as his thumbs moved up to pinch and tease her nipples. She felt them harden into tight, throbbing nubs. Each flick of his thumbs sent another thrill skittering along her nerve endings. The exquisite lightning bolts of pleasure he coaxed from her nipples sizzled all the way through her, calling up an answering flare from her very core.

His erection grew even harder, if that were possible. It pulsed with energy, with his need. Her own need overwhelmed her, sending rationality flying right out of her head.

So much for getting over him. She tossed her head back as the last dregs of caution chased after those rational thoughts.

Ash growled deep in his throat, and lifted his head to kiss her, but she was still caught up in the sparks his thumbs were striking at her breasts. When she didn't meet his kiss, he put his hand around her neck and pulled her down. Utterly defeated by his strength and intensity, she lowered her mouth to his and kissed him softly.

For a few seconds he kept the kiss sweet and soft, but then he increased the pressure and his tongue traced the seam of her lips until she parted them. He slid his hand up to cradle the back of her head and took her mouth with his—hard, deep, his tongue thrusting insistently, sensually to meet hers.

Her heart was racing so fast that it took her breath, and her whole body pulsed with desire, but still he kissed her. He was relentless, his taking of her mouth just short of brutal. She put her hands against his chest for support as she gave herself up to the feel of his mouth and tongue.

Too soon, he pulled back, stopping the kisses as suddenly as he'd started. But all he did was change his target. He trailed his tongue down along her jaw and farther, to the hollow just above her collarbone, where he nibbled and suckled lightly.

His fingers followed his lips, touching her with the same erotic charge as his mouth. Then he moved both lips and fingertips farther down, trailing fire along the top of her already ultra-sensitized breast.

Before she could take a full breath, his fingers were on her nipple again. It tightened even more until it ached with exquisite, nearly painful pleasure.

Then he took the throbbing nub into his mouth, and what she'd thought was pleasure grew and expanded until she knew she would explode. She arched, pushing her breast into his mouth as the liquid fire burned all the way through her.

He gasped, and she felt cool air shiver across her wet, aching nipple. His erection pressed against her, nearly undoing her.

She threw her head back and moaned. Then her hands were desperately pulling at the hem of his T-shirt. She pushed it up, baring his abs and chest. Determined to make him suffer the same agonizing pleasure he was giving her, she bent her head and kissed each of his nipples in turn. Then she scraped her teeth along one of them.

The feel of her teeth grazing the surprisingly sensitive tip sent fierce shudders through Ash's body. His buttocks tightened and he thrust forward, clenching his jaw against a groan.

She moved to the other nipple, squeezing it between her teeth, nibbling at it, sucking on it until he thought he would surely come just from the exquisite aching pleasure of her mouth on him. The feeling was peculiar—definitely erotic but also disconcerting, as if his male nipples shouldn't be sensitive like a woman's were.

"Rach, don't do that," he said hoarsely, fisting his hand in her hair.

She laughed deep in her throat and the vibration added another layer of pleasure, driving him even closer to orgasm.

"Be careful," he groaned. "I'm getting—too close."

She lifted her head and pinned him with what he could only describe as a wicked, hooded gaze. She licked her lips and smiled, then bent down again.

He steeled himself for more strangely erotic sensations,

but she didn't return to his nipples. She had a new target in mind. Her fingers reached for the button and zipper on his jeans. He pushed her hands away, sucked in his breath and undid them himself. As he slid them down his legs, cool air shivered across his hot, pulsing erection.

Then she touched him, her small hand soft but firm as she squeezed him, creating a new, more unbearable friction than the stiff material of his jeans. He thrust against her hand, rigidly holding on to his control.

Rachel's breasts were bare, her little pajama top already pushed up to give him access. He gently positioned her until she was sitting upright atop him and slid his hand down to the swell of her hip.

She lifted herself so he could slide her pajama bottoms down. When he got them past her bottom, she stretched out along his length so he could push them off. They'd always fallen into a natural rhythm, their foreplay in sync, their climaxes close if not simultaneous. But right now, in this erotic place, they were like two parts of the same whole. They moved in concert, as if they'd always been together.

Her hand stroked him again, and his thoughts dissipated. All that mattered was sensation.

He heard and felt her panting. Her chest rose and fell rapidly, her breaths coming in short, sharp bursts, aligning with his.

She was turned on. She wanted this as much as he did. And that was a lot. More than he ever had before.

As they moved together in the ancient dance of lovers, he was aware, without actually thinking, that she was sexier, softer, more womanly than she'd been before. Her breasts were fuller, heavier in his hands, the nipples larger and darker.

Because she was pregnant.

The thought hit him square in the face. For a split second, reality trumped even his sizzling desire, and fear stole his breath and nearly deflated his erection.

She was pregnant, and neither of their lives would be the same again. What was wrong with him? He was acting like a randy teen, rather than a responsible man in his thirties.

For a desperate instant, he wanted to push her away. Apologize to her and tell her that he was wrong to start things up again. Certainly hadn't intended to give her the idea that he wanted to be with her and their baby. *Did he?*

He closed his eyes and drew in a long breath. He was supposed to be her protector—her temporary protector, not her once and future lover. Not to mention he had a job to do—find the man who had killed his parents.

He realized he'd gone perfectly still. Realized Rachel had, too. She was staring down at him, fear almost smothering the desire in her eyes.

He blinked and realized that right now, all he cared about was stoking the flaming desire he'd seen in her green-gold eyes. He didn't want to watch it die—didn't want to be the one who did that to her. So he took her hand and, watching her carefully, moved it back to his erection.

For an endless moment, she didn't move, just stared at him with those wide, innocent eyes. Then slowly, she lowered her gaze and began to stroke him again. At first softly, barely brushing his flesh. Then more strongly, more urgently, until he was holding on to the dregs of control with all his strength.

Ignoring the last passing reminder of the inevitable regret he was doomed to face in the morning, he took her in his arms and held her as he flipped them both on the couch.

He hovered over her, his weight on his arms, and kissed her until he could think of nothing but sinking into her, like he'd done so many times before.

He'd missed her. Missed making love with her. Missed the feel of her beneath him. Missed her wide-eyed, oddly colored gaze on him as she waited for him to fill and fulfill her.

He slid his hand up her thigh and delved into her with a finger. She arched upward, pressing her breasts into his chest.

"Ash," she whispered. "Please—"

He knew what she was asking. Her hand closed around him, squeezing, rubbing, caressing. "Please—"

He raised himself above her and pushed into her silken, waiting core. And groaned as her hot, wet flesh took him in and clamped around him.

Rachel cried out softly, then arched her hips, giving him full access, which he took. He moved slowly, excruciatingly slowly, giving her time to get used to him. He tortured himself, holding back, until he thought he might explode.

Rachel lay there, waiting for a few seconds, but then she moaned in frustration. She didn't want it slow and easy. He laughed softly. More contradiction. Wide-eyed innocence paired with ravenous desire.

"Okay, Rach," he whispered in her ear, then kissed his way down her jaw to her lips. "Here we go."

Then he lifted and thrust—hard. Hard and long. He pulled back until he was nearly out, then thrust again. And again. All the time he watched her, held her gaze, until he saw her expression change. Saw her mouth open in that little O he loved to see because that meant she was just about to tip over that final obstacle to ecstasy.

Then she did. She gasped and arched as her body contracted around him in quick, rhythmic pulses. He gave one more deep thrust and came in a burst of inner light that blinded him like sheet lightning in a summer thunderstorm. And like sheet lightning, it went on and on. And on.

Finally, drained, he buried his face in the hollow of her shoulder and gasped for breath. Her chest was rising and falling, and her body occasionally shook in a tiny shudder, little aftershocks of her orgasm.

She sighed softly and brushed her fingers languidly along the nape of his neck, then down his back.

After a while, he didn't know how long, he finally gathered the strength to lift his head. He gazed into her eyes. She gazed back, her face relaxed, her lips slightly parted. He brushed her lips, feeling her warm breath on his skin. Then he lay on his side with his back against the couch cushions and pulled her close.

She settled in with a soft sigh, as if she was made to fit there.

RACHEL LAY IN ASH'S ARMS, listening to his long, slow breaths. She'd been surprised by the intensity of his lovemaking. Almost as surprised as she was that he'd even started it. Almost as surprised as she'd been to wake up in his arms.

He'd been so casual when they'd dated before. Yes, they'd been together nearly every day for four months. Yes, he'd satisfied her more than anyone she'd ever slept with—okay, than the *two* other men she'd ever slept with.

But tonight he'd been a very different lover. He'd been serious, intense, and in a way, sweeter and more considerate than he'd ever been in the past. Tonight his lovemaking had devastated her, because she knew that when he woke up, he'd regret it.

He barely stirred as she slid quietly out of his arms and off the couch. She picked up her pajamas and slipped them on, then turned toward the guest bedroom. But she was too warm and her head was spinning with all the events of the past couple of weeks, and especially tonight. *READ HERE*

OK She glanced out the window, then at Ash. He was sound asleep, his lips parted and his breaths deep and even. She didn't want to wake him, but she'd sure like to get some fresh air and clear her head. She stepped into the foyer and carefully unlatched the front door.

She tiptoed across the porch to the glider and sat down. The air was cool—the crisp coolness of fall with its promise of winter that was so different from the soft coolness of spring. She took a deep breath that turned into a yawn.

If she had a blanket, she could fall asleep out here, she thought, then chuckled. Like she'd told Ash earlier, she could fall asleep just about anywhere except in bed where she ought to be. She wondered what time it was. Late, she knew. Maybe even close to morning.

Morning. A weight settled on her chest. She dreaded facing Ash in the morning. He'd be irritable and uncomfortable. His head would be spinning with all that had happened to him—a lot of it because of her.

She didn't know this serious, worried Ash, who was being forced to accept that the man who'd been behind bars for twenty years for the murder of his parents was innocent. This Ash, who was furious with her for her part in freeing Campbell, and suspicious of her for turning up pregnant with his child.

At least he hadn't tried to deny that he was the baby's father. She was sure he remembered the night the baby was conceived as clearly as she did. That night in New Orleans when they'd been so hungry for each other—laughing and teasing as they finished their deceptively fruity Hurricanes in those huge souvenir glasses.

She lay her hand across her tummy. She couldn't regret

that their carelessness had created a child, although she knew he did.

A flash of light caught her attention. She glanced up and saw the headlights of a car turning onto Ash's street. But as she squinted, idly wondering who was coming home this late—or early—the headlights went out.

That was odd. She could see the vehicle, reflecting the dim light from the streetlamps. It was still moving, creeping along in the darkness.

The corner of her mouth quirked up in a little smile. Whoever it was, he must be seriously sneaking in late.

Shrinking back into the corner of the glider so she wouldn't be seen, Rachel peered through the bushes in Ash's yard, watching the car with casual interest. She was ready to go inside, but she didn't want to move and call attention to herself. She'd rather stay put until the driver parked and disappeared into his house.

While she watched, she entertained herself by imagining who he was and what he'd been doing. And of course, if he were a man or a woman. Was it a teenager who'd stayed out way too late and was trying to sneak in without Mom knowing? *Good luck with that.*

Or a husband out playing poker or drinking with the guys? And was he sneaking in because he didn't want the neighbors to know how he spent his nights, or because he didn't want to wake his wife?

The vehicle rounded the cul-de-sac without stopping. Rachel squinted again. Maybe it was a police car casing the street, making sure everything was quiet. But she didn't see lights on top of the car or reflective lettering on the side.

To her surprise and trepidation, the car pulled up in front of Ash's house and stopped without cutting the engine. Rachel's senses went on alert and her shoulders hunched with tension as she tried to make herself as small as possible.

Her pulse began to pound. This was no delinquent teen or guilty husband. This person who'd sneaked into the subdivision in the middle of the night was not there for some innocent reason. She listened intently, ready to bolt inside if the car's engine turned off.

But it didn't. It looked like the driver planned to be there for a while. It had to be someone watching her or Ash.

Had Uncle Charlie—Chief Hammond—assigned an unmarked car to keep an eye on her because of the break-in? No. He wouldn't do that. The department was already shorthanded. Besides, she was sure he knew she was with one of his detectives.

Maybe he'd assigned someone to watch Ash. Was he worried Ash would do something stupid like go vigilante, looking for the real killer?

Then a scary thought hit her. What if it was the real murderer, alerted by the press conference? With Rick Campbell declared innocent, the police would reopen the case. Rachel tried to follow her sudden thought with rational reasoning.

Why would the killer be watching Ash? Because he was a police detective? Maybe the killer knew that the police had something that pointed to him.

If so, Ash's life could be in danger. And she was trapped out here. If she tried calling out to Ash, the driver might hear her and get to her before Ash could.

Was that the most rational explanation? The vehicle was parked directly in front of Ash's house. Pretty obvious, if he were watching them.

On the other hand, it could be just a jealous boyfriend or a stalker, watching someone else who lived near Ash?

If *she* were stalking somebody, she wouldn't be so obvious as to park right in front of their house. She'd park somewhere else, so if she were noticed, she could get away before they reached her car, or she could claim to be waiting for someone.

She decided she wouldn't be a very good stalker. She wasn't creative enough for plausible deniability.

Still, no matter who it was or why they were here, they'd effectively trapped her in this dark corner of the porch until they decided to leave. And *now* she was sleepy. *No.* She couldn't fall asleep now. But her pregnant body had other ideas. She fought her heavy eyelids, but ultimately lost.

When a noise startled her, she realized she'd been dozing. The noise was the car pulling away. The sky was beginning to lighten. She sat up carefully, squinting at the car's license plate. She could see most of it—enough that she was pretty sure a friend of hers in the DMV could tell her who it was registered to.

The car, which had been creeping away from the curb, stopped. Rachel froze, holding her breath. Had he seen her? The sky was barely light enough to signal the streetlamps to go off, and she was in shadow at the dark end of the porch, and partially hidden by shrubs, but she had moved, trying to get a better look at the license plate.

She tensed, prepared to scream if the driver got out and came her way, but a garage door screeched open a few doors down and the mysterious car moved on.

Rachel breathed a sigh of relief. Once the car disappeared around a corner, she got up and slipped inside. Ash was still asleep on the couch, so she tiptoed into the guest room and glanced at the clock on the dresser. It was after six. She looked longingly at the bed, then decided she should probably go ahead and get ready for work.

She gingerly touched the cut on her head. It wasn't

nearly as sore, and that was good, because she couldn't wait another day to wash her hair.

As she grabbed underwear and clothes, she argued with herself about telling Ash what she'd seen. She didn't want to tell him anything until she'd run the license plate. He needed to know that someone might be watching the house, but if she could present him with the whole package—make and model of car, license plate and the car's registrant, maybe she could redeem herself a little in his eyes.

Chapter Ten

The sound of a door closing woke Ash. He blinked. Rachel must be up. He stirred and realized he was lying on the couch, naked. And alone.

He sure hadn't been alone last night. He could still smell the subtle coconut essence that always scented her skin. He closed his eyes as his body reacted to the memories—the taste of her skin, the feel of her mouth on his, the eagerness with which she'd slid right into his arms. They'd fallen into the rhythm that made sex with her so erotic, so satisfying.

Even more satisfying last night, because her body seemed softer and firmer at the same time. Her breasts were fuller, more luscious than he remembered.

Because she was pregnant.

Oh, hell. What kind of idiot was he, to fall back into bed with her? He was *so* not ready for that kind of responsibility. Not that he had a choice. She was pregnant and he was—what?

Angry? No. It was just as much his fault as hers. Takes two, as they say.

Nope. Scared spitless was more like it. And overwhelmed. How was he going to deal with her pregnancy and solving his parents' murder all at the same time?

Sighing, he glanced at his watch. It was after six. He

might as well go ahead and shower. No way was he getting back to sleep.

He got up, grabbed his clothes and headed toward his room. He almost made it, too, but just as he stepped to his door, the guest room door opened and Rachel came out, heading for the hall bath.

She stopped, startled, when she saw him. "Oh!" she said, staring at his nakedness.

"Hey," he said. "Where'd you disappear to?" Without thinking, he reached out to push a fallen strand of hair off her forehead. She drew back, just enough that his hand touched nothing but air.

"I couldn't sleep." She avoided his gaze, avoided looking in his direction at all.

He smiled wryly. "Sorry," he said. "If I'd known you were up—"

She bit her lip. "That's—okay. I'm just going to—" She gestured toward the bathroom.

"Go ahead. I'll make coffee."

Nodding, she ducked her head and slipped through the bathroom door and closed it behind her.

So, that took care of that question. From the way she acted, Rachel obviously regretted the night before more than he did. He tossed his T-shirt and underwear onto the master bathroom floor and pulled on his jeans, then went into the kitchen to make coffee.

His thoughts slammed him in the face like an unexpected echo. *Regretted?* Something about that word stopped him cold.

Maybe Rachel regretted what they'd done, but although he knew his loss of control the night before had been a really bad idea, he couldn't regret it. Sex with her had always been surprisingly erotic.

Damn it. He had enough on his plate right now without

the complication of a renewed relationship with the one woman he hadn't been able to get out of his mind.

He'd just fixed himself a cup of coffee when he heard Rachel turn off the water. Taking his cup with him, he headed into his bathroom to shower and shave.

By the time he emerged, clean and combed and dressed for work, Rachel was sitting at his kitchen table, sipping at a glass of ice water. She was dressed, and her hair was damp. She had on makeup although he didn't know why she bothered. He thought she looked better without it.

"No coffee?" he asked, holding up his cup.

She nodded toward her glass. "Pregnant—and nauseous," she said, her voice slightly raspy.

He refilled his cup, then leaned against the counter. "I guess we should talk about that."

She eyed him narrowly. *"That?"* she echoed. "You mean this?" she said archly, pointing at her stomach and shaking her head. "There's nothing to talk about."

"Nothing to talk about? Of course there is."

She was shaking her head. "No. I mean, listen to you. You think of your child as *that*."

"Rach, I don't think of—" He stopped when she lifted her chin pugnaciously. "I've got a lot on my plate right now. I need to concentrate on finding the man who murdered my parents. I'd like to know what you intend to do, so I don't have to worry about it." He knew as soon as the words left his mouth that he'd said the wrong thing.

Rachel stiffened. She stood and picked up her glass. "Please, Ash, don't worry about *it*. I am perfectly happy— in fact, I prefer—to have and rear my child myself. He doesn't need a father who has too much on his plate, and whose dating habits are prime watercooler conversation." She walked past him out of the kitchen, her back straight and her head high.

In a couple of minutes she reappeared, carrying her purse and her overnight bag. She marched straight to the front door without even glancing his way, unlatched it and left.

Ash stared at the door until he heard her car start up and drive away. He lifted his cup to his mouth, then grimaced. Suddenly the coffee was bitter and cold. His mouth curled wryly. He didn't miss the metaphor. He turned off the coffeemaker and grabbed his keys.

"Good job, Kendall," he muttered. "That went well."

RACHEL HAD CALMED DOWN a little by the time she got to her desk. Her chest still burned with anger, though. She should have known that Ash hadn't meant what he'd said last night. His declaration that he wanted to be there for his child was obviously just a ploy to get into her pants. And of course it worked.

She needed to get out of his apartment. Having him so close ripped away her protective shields. What an idiot she was. Leave it to her to fall in love with Ashanova.

Anger swelled again, this time at herself. One good thing about fury, it knocked the queasiness right out of her. Still, she nibbled on crackers and sipped cold water as she ran through her email and edited an analysis report that Neil Chasen was waiting for.

When she called Detective Chasen to let him know the report was ready, she asked him about her apartment.

"I was going to give Kendall a call this morning. We've released it as a crime scene, and the cleanup crew has finished. As far as SLMPD is concerned, you can get in there and get clothes or whatever."

"Thank goodness! I'll be back home tonight."

"I thought you were going to stay with Kendall for a while, just to be safe."

"No," she said shortly, then continued. "I haven't seen a DNA report from my case. Didn't any trace evidence show up?"

"A couple of hairs, but we didn't get a hit in CODIS."

She sighed. "That's so frustrating."

"Yeah. Listen, if you notice that anything else is missing—other than that DNA report, let me know. Meanwhile, I've been ordered to turn this over to the task force looking into the Christmas Eve Murders."

"Oh. Do they understand that he must have followed me when I delivered that report? Otherwise, how would he know I had a copy? They need to check the security cameras around the commissioner's office."

"I can't tell you what they're going to do. It's all very hush-hush."

Dismay flooded her, but she lifted her chin. "I understand. Thanks, Neil," she said.

Then she remembered the car she'd seen the night before. She'd been so angry at Ash, she'd forgotten to mention it.

"I said, I'll be over to pick up that report in a few minutes."

Rachel hung up and then dialed her friend in the Department of Motor Vehicles. "Can you run a license plate for me?" she asked, then provided the tag number. "It's a Missouri plate."

"Sure," her friend said. "You owe me lunch."

"You got it. We'll get together next week sometime."

"Sounds great."

"You'll call me with the info?" Rachel asked.

"Actually I've got it right here, unless you need an official report."

"Not right now. I just want to find out whose name is on that registration."

"The name is Campbell."

Her friend said more, but Rachel didn't hear it. Her brain zeroed in on the name *Campbell*. It *was* Rick Campbell. The name could not be a coincidence.

Rick Campbell was stalking Ash.

ASH WAS CALLED OUT TO A home invasion shooting just as he was pulling out of his driveway. That plus finishing a few reports took him all morning. Just as he was about to go to lunch, he got a call from the officer who'd done the canvassing of Rachel's apartment building.

"Nobody saw a red compact," he told Ash. "I couldn't find anybody who'd seen anything."

Ash sighed. "Thanks for rechecking," he said. He hung up and called Devin. "Hey," he said when his brother answered. "How's everything?"

"You mean other than finding out Campbell's innocent and dealing with Uncle Craig's breakdown?"

"Breakdown?" Ash repeated, surprised. "What happened?"

Devin sighed through the phone line. "It's not literally a breakdown, although I wonder what a psychiatrist would say if he talked to him. I've never seen him like this."

"Yeah, the other night I thought he was going to have a stroke, he was so mad."

"I don't know, Ash. This doesn't seem as much like anger as it does fear. I think he's scared to death."

"Of what?" Ash asked.

"That's what I can't figure out. I'm angry and worried, especially about Natalie. But Uncle Craig's reaction—it's just bizarre," Dev said. "I actually considered making him go to the hospital."

"Well, they've assigned a task force to reopen the case.

I just hope they find the real murderer fast, for all our sakes."

"Yeah. Me, too. This is ridiculous. It's been twenty years, and suddenly we're right back in the middle of it."

Devin paused. "Have you talked to Thad?"

"Not since the press conference," Ash said. "I left a message letting him know that Campbell has been released, but he hasn't gotten back to me."

"Maybe we should contact the magazine?"

"He told me that he'd be home as soon as he can catch a ride." Ash took a long breath.

"Dev, that night—we've never really talked about it much. Was Natalie screaming the first thing you heard?"

"That's right. I'd just gotten in. I thought she was screaming with excitement—Christmas morning, you know." Devin cleared his throat. "But then it hit me that she was literally screaming in fear."

"Your bedroom was closest to the parents' wing. You didn't hear the glass break or the gunshot?"

Devin sighed in exasperation. "I told you, no. Nat's screams were the first thing I heard."

"Did you remember that Dad was killed by a gunshot?" Ash asked.

"Yeah, sure. Why?"

"I didn't, not until last night. It's strange that the man shot him but strangled Mom."

Devin cleared his throat. "Yeah. I remember the policeman—I guess it was Hammond, saying he probably didn't want to shoot twice, afraid somebody would hear it."

"That makes no sense whatsoever."

"Ash, our parents were murdered on Christmas Eve. What about any of it *does* make sense?"

"Yeah. Let me know how Uncle Craig's doing," Ash said, then hung up.

He walked down the hall to Chief Hammond's glassed-in office. The interior blinds were open and Ash could see the chief at his desk, reading a report. He rapped on the door.

Hammond looked up and gestured for Ash to come in. "What's up, Detective?"

"I'd like to ask a few more questions about the murder."

Hammond set aside the report and frowned at him. "The murder? You mean your parents' murders? I thought we covered that. I still say that the DNA was contaminated. Campbell was guilty then and he's guilty now."

"Rachel told me if the sample was contaminated it would have DNA from two different people. It would be obvious."

Hammond leaned forward. "Not if somebody switched the samples. I've got a couple of buddies on the task force. They'll take another look at the DNA. Maybe have an independent lab run it." Hammond picked up a pencil off his desk and fiddled with it. "They met yesterday for the first time."

"One of the members told you that they're going to rerun the DNA?"

"They've had one meeting. They haven't talked about it yet, but they will. I'll guarantee you."

Ash wondered if Hammond really had influence with the task force, as he was implying. "I've been thinking about some things," he said carefully. He didn't want to give the chief any hint that he'd been reading the case files. "I know you said the case was open-and-shut, but it seems like there were a lot of loose ends."

"Loose ends?" Hammond glared at him. "What the hell are you talking about? Loose ends, my ass."

Ash shifted in his chair. He'd already put Hammond on the defensive. He doubted there was any way to avoid it, but he had hoped to get in some questions first. "Well, I'm sure the task force will address them. It's just a few things that never got answered, like what happened to my mother's ring."

Hammond narrowed one eye and his brow furrowed. "Right. The ring. We figured Campbell dropped it. A shame we never found it for you kids."

Ash nodded. "And the gun. It never turned up, either."

"Guns are probably the easiest thing in the world to get rid of. Hell, there were two ponds and a creek between your folks' house and where we picked up Campbell."

Hammond got up and paced in front of the windows. Ash had to turn in his chair.

"Have you looked at the newspapers from back then?" Hammond asked.

"My aunt Angie saved them, I think, but no. I haven't."

"You ought to. There was a public outcry like nothing I've ever seen. Your parents were prominent in the business community and among the social set. The whole city was up in arms, wanting justice. We were afraid there might actually be riots."

Ash nodded. "I remember something about a second prowler. That Campbell said he saw a man running from the area of the mansion. Did you look into that at all?" As soon as the words were out of his mouth, he knew he'd gone too far. Hammond's neck turned a splotchy red, and the color crept up to stain his face.

"I'm gonna ask you again, Detective Kendall. What the hell are you talking about?" His voice grew louder. "Are you suggesting I fell down on the job? I've cut you a lot of slack because of how your folks died, but you're treading on thin ice here."

Glancing out through the inner glass walls of Hammond's office, Ash saw that people in the outer office had turned and were looking at them. Hammond's voice had risen enough that it could be heard outside the room.

Ash held up his hands. "I'm not suggesting—I know that twenty years ago you didn't have all the tools we have nowadays," he said. Hammond could make his job a living hell if he wanted to, and Ash did not want to antagonize him.

While Ash was speaking, Hammond closed the blinds. Then he stood over him. He took a long breath, then another one, obviously trying to calm himself. "We checked out every lead, every wacko phone call and habitual confessor. My men didn't find a single footprint from that night except Campbell's. Now, I get that you're upset, son. I am, too. But by God, Campbell's guilty," he said, jabbing the air with the pencil. "And one way or another, he'll pay. I may not be on that task force, but I'm still the best detective you ever saw."

He sat back down behind his desk. "Now get the hell out of here before I get angry and fire you."

Ash got out. He'd hoped that talking to Hammond would make him feel better about the reopened investigation of his parents' murders, but it didn't.

All it did was fill his head with more questions. It sounded like Hammond had covered all the bases. What if Hammond hadn't found Campbell conveniently burglarizing homes in the neighborhood? What if he'd been forced to look farther for a suspect?

A week ago, if he'd even thought about it, Ash would have been naively assured that his parents' murderer was behind bars. He had issues, as did his brothers and sister, stemming from that traumatic event. But at least he hadn't been tortured by the knowledge that the man who'd viciously murdered his mom and dad was out there somewhere, free.

Chapter Eleven

It was almost five o'clock. People would be headed home for the evening, and Rachel hadn't tracked down Rick Campbell's address yet. She hung up her lab coat, made sure the lab doors were locked and headed upstairs.

Ever since she'd found out that the car she'd seen the night before belonged to Mrs. Martha Campbell, Rick's mother, she'd been thinking about what she was going to do. Then, right in the middle of a procedure to isolate DNA from a hair sample, it had hit her.

She had the information in her desk. The unsanitized report, that the commissioner's chief of staff had handed her just before the press conference, had addresses listed.

Back at her desk, she retrieved the report from her file drawer. She laid the report on her desk as she glanced around. Almost everyone was gone. Vanessa had left before Rachel had gotten upstairs, and Jack and Frank, the other criminalists, were at a crime scene.

She opened the folder and right there, at the top of the form, Campbell's parents' address was filled in. Rachel got out her phone and entered the address and phone number into it. Then she scanned the rest of the form. In a section labeled *Other Address* was Rick's address. While the top part of the form was computer generated, Rick's address had been filled in with a pen.

"Yes!" Rachel whispered, and entered the address, which was an apartment not far from his parents' home, into her phone. There was no separate phone number listed.

Just as she inputted the last digits, she heard footsteps. She closed the folder as Ash walked around the corner.

"Hey," he said with a small smile.

She picked up the folder as casually as she could and stuck in back into the open file drawer. "Hi," she replied.

"I thought I'd see how you're doing."

"I'm fine. I was just about to leave."

"Yeah. I figured you might be. D'you want to grab some dinner?"

Rachel frowned. What was he up to? Had he talked to Neil? The way she'd left it this morning, she'd figured she might have to get a hotel room, but now that she knew her apartment was clear and clean, she was planning to go back there. She'd packed up everything, making absolutely sure she wasn't leaving a thing behind, not even a tissue, this time. "Why?"

Ash rubbed the back of his neck. "I'd like to have a chance to apologize for being a jerk this morning." He stepped closer to her.

She fought the urge to step backward. When he was too close to her, she couldn't think clearly.

"I do want to be involved, Rachel. That's my—" He stopped. "I'm the baby's father, and I want to go with you to your doctor's appointments and help you with—the breathing classes or whatever."

She laughed. She couldn't help it. "You have no clue what you're talking about, do you?" she said.

He shook his head, his mouth quirking into a rueful smile. "No. I really don't."

"Or what you're getting yourself into."

"That either. But I want to know." He sighed. "Look, can we just talk about it? Over dinner?"

Rachel regarded him. He was more handsome than one man had a right to be. He was smart, wealthy and basically a good guy, even if he did have commitment issues. She and her baby could have done a lot worse.

And she knew she would let him be a part of their baby's life. She wouldn't deny him the joys and the heartaches she knew they were both in for, raising a child. But right now, she was only eight—now nine—weeks pregnant. She didn't have to let him off the hook quite yet.

Besides, she had plans for tonight.

"I don't think so, Ash. Not tonight."

He seemed taken aback, as if he hadn't even considered that she'd refuse. "Oh. But you're coming ho—you're coming back to the house, right?"

She shook her head. "No. Neil told me my apartment has been cleared. I'm going home." She slid her phone into her purse and stood.

"But whoever broke into your house is still out there. You might not be safe."

She shrugged. "I'm not concerned. I do have a gun. And from now on, I'm going to keep it with me. If anything happens, I'll be armed."

Ash's jaw dropped. "No, Rachel. You can't do that."

"Why not? If I'd had my gun with me when that man broke into my apartment, he'd be in jail and I wouldn't have a scar on my head." Her hand drifted up toward the cut, which was still sore.

His face darkened. "No. That's not the way it works. It's dangerous for a—for you to keep a loaded gun in your apartment."

"I'm not going to shoot myself," she countered.

"Statistics show that people who have guns in their

homes are more likely to be shot. It's not as easy as you might think to actually pull the trigger, knowing you could kill another person."

"I know. Someone hesitates and the intruder takes the gun away from them and shoots them with it. I've already heard all this from my dad. And my mom. Mom's like you—she thinks I'll just end up having my gun taken away from me. Dad, on the other hand, taught me how not to let that happen. Trust me. I'm very well trained."

"What are you going to do? Sit there behind your door with your gun in your hand, waiting for someone to break in? I can't stand by and let you do that."

She smiled. "You can't stop me. It's a free country and I have a carry permit. If you don't believe I can handle a gun, ask Uncle Charlie. He was at the range a lot of times while Dad was teaching me everything he knew. He knows how good I am."

"Fine." Ash held up his hands. "Whatever you want to do. When you decide you're ready to talk about what role I get to play in our baby's life, you give me a call."

"Fine," she responded.

He turned on his heel and pushed open the doors. "And try not to shoot yourself," he snapped, and stalked away.

BACK AT HIS HOUSE, Ash paced and grumbled to himself. He'd been stunned that Rachel had turned down his invitation to dinner. She'd surprised him, first by saying she had other plans, then by declaring that she was going to go armed from now on.

He didn't think he'd ever met anyone that stubborn. It had taken a lot for him to go to her and apologize. Not that he didn't regret being harsh with her. He did. It just wasn't that easy for him to admit when he'd made a mistake.

It didn't help that he found himself in a situation he'd

never been in before. When it came to women, he'd always been the one in charge. The one who decided when to heat up a relationship and when to cool it down.

But from the very beginning, Rachel had been different. They'd spent weekends at his home, which broke one of his cardinal rules. He never spent the night with a woman, not at her place and not at his.

Nor had he ever taken a woman away for a weekend, but before he realized what he'd been doing, he'd asked Rachel to go to New Orleans with him for an idyllic few days.

And he sure as hell had never slipped up and gotten a woman pregnant.

From the beginning, Rachel had perplexed him. He'd come back from that weekend so terrified by how much he loved being with her that he'd broken up with her two weeks later. But he was too late. Rachel was pregnant and he was a father.

WHEN THE ALARM CLOCK rang at seven-thirty that evening, Rachel jumped. She hadn't realized she'd been asleep. But she must have been, because she remembered sitting behind a giant door, picking off soldier ants with her Glock as they crawled through.

Shaking her head to rid herself of the odd dream, she stood up. She got so tired these days. Rubbing her tummy, she whispered, "And it's all your fault," to the tiny baby growing inside her.

She'd hurried home from work and set the alarm for seven-thirty, not even dreaming that she'd actually fall asleep. She'd wanted to wait until after the dinner hour to go see Rick Campbell, because she didn't want to take a chance of missing him. She had his address, but she had no idea if he had a job.

She wasn't totally convinced that going to see him was a good idea, but she wanted, for Ash's sake, to ask why he'd been sitting outside Ash's house in the early morning hours. Once she knew, then she could tell Ash, because, as he'd just told her the other night, he had too much on his plate right now. He didn't need something else to worry about.

By the time those thoughts had gone through her head, she'd put her shoes on and combed her hair and was ready to go. She hadn't had dinner, but she grabbed some crackers and a bottle of water.

Just as she was about to head out the door, her phone rang. She thought for a second of letting the machine pick up, but then she sighed and answered it.

"Ms. Stevens?"

She sighed. Most of the time if the caller addressed her as Ms. Stevens rather than Dr. Stevens, it was a wily telemarketer that had sneaked past the no-call list. It for sure was not someone she knew. "Yes?" she said impatiently.

"This is—uh—Rick Campbell."

Rachel's heart jumped and her hand flew to her mouth. The next breath she took was a struggle, because her chest was suddenly tight. She swallowed and tried to get control of her breathing. "Yes?"

"I hate to bother you, but is there any way I could talk to you? Ask you some questions?"

She didn't know what to say. Rick Campbell's situation was different from anything she'd ever dealt with before. Her standard answer to reporters, suspects, even victims, was that she was unable to comment on an open case. But Campbell's case was closed.

"What—what about?" she rasped, because she couldn't think of a reason to deny him. And she really did want to know what he was calling about.

"It's about the—the DNA and my case and everything. I gotta tell you I'm worried."

She bit her lower lip, wondering what she should do. Was she still obligated to refuse to talk to him? Did she even want to ask that question of herself? After all, she'd been on her way out the door to see him when he'd called.

"I don't think you have anything to worry about, Mr. Campbell."

"I'll meet you in a public place. I'll come to your office. Whatever I need to do," Campbell said, sounding desperate.

"Mr. Campbell, I have to ask you a question. Do you drive a red Ford Focus?"

He didn't speak for a beat. "My mom's letting me use hers."

"Have you been watching Detective Kendall?"

There was a pause on the other end of the phone. Rachel was afraid Campbell would hang up without answering, but after a few seconds she heard him sigh.

"I—I don't want to scare you or anything, Ms. Stevens. You saved my life. I was—I was following you. I've been working at a bar. Didn't get off 'til it closed at 2:00 a.m."

"You've got a job?" Rachel asked. He'd only been out of prison for a week or so.

"Uh, yeah. The D.A. put in a word for me."

"So why would you take the chance that somebody seeing an idling car in front of their home at two or later in the morning might call the police?"

"I just wanted to—I felt close to you, you know? But you were with him and I know he hates me. I was afraid he'd send me back to jail."

"Detective Kendall? He's not going to do that. You've been cleared. You're a free man now."

Rachel heard a snort. "Yeah, you'd think so. Sometimes I think I was better off in jail."

"You don't mean that."

"You might be surprised," he said. "Okay, now that you know I was following you, are you afraid to meet me?"

She was a little apprehensive, but Campbell sounded more desperate and fearful than vengeful. Still, a public place was probably a good idea. "Do you have time tomorrow afternoon? What time do you go to work?" she asked.

"Yeah, sure. I'm not working today or tomorrow. Today's my day off and tomorrow I've got an interview for a permanent job."

"There's a coffee shop on Market Street near the mall. It's called The Whole Bean Thing. Do you know it?"

Campbell laughed shortly. "Nope, but I can find it."

Rachel grimaced. Of course he didn't know the shop. He'd been in prison for almost half his life. "I'll be wearing—"

"I know what you look like, Ms. Stevens."

"Right. The press conference. Okay, then. I'll see you at five o'clock?" She could leave work a few minutes early to meet him.

"Sure. That works. Thanks."

Rachel hung up. That was weird. And fortuitous. Rick Campbell had said he was worried about the DNA and his case. Was he afraid that being cleared of the crime after twenty years was too good to be true?

Had he really been out in front of Ash's house to watch *her*, not him? And was his reason really so innocent?

She squeezed her eyes shut and rubbed her temples. She was getting a headache from not eating, and the stars were beginning to spark at the edge of her vision.

She quit trying to figure out why Campbell wanted to

see her and instead, went to her refrigerator and opened the door. Her choices for dinner were ham that had been there since the day of her attack, cheese that had been there for at least a month and eggs that she was sure would float.

Sighing, she closed the refrigerator door, picked up the phone and pressed a preset number. "I'd like to order a medium pizza with everything but anchovies, please," she said, looking at her watch. She'd eat, then go to bed. She needed her rest, because tomorrow was going to be a very interesting day.

While she waited for the pizza, she took out her Glock and cleaned it. It wouldn't hurt for her to have it with her when she met Campbell tomorrow.

The next day, Rachel sat in the coffee shop holding her purse on her lap. It had become uncomfortably heavy, but she wasn't about to set it on the floor. Not with the Glock positioned within easy reach inside it. Although she'd talked big to Ash about having a carry permit and everything her father had taught her about using and caring for her weapon, this was the first time she'd ever gone out in public packing. Like she'd told Ash, she'd always carried her weapon in the trunk of her car.

She took a sip of her now cold decaf latte and looked for the twentieth time at the clock over the barista's head. It was almost six and Rick Campbell hadn't shown up.

For the first half hour, Rachel had given him the benefit of the doubt. He was stuck in traffic. He'd gotten a late start. His job interview was a half hour away.

But now she had to assume that he wasn't coming. Why had he set her up to meet him if he wasn't going to show? Fear curdled the latte in her stomach. Had he wanted to get her out of the way so he could get to Ash? She shook her head. That didn't make sense, because he'd called her home phone number, so he knew she was back in her apartment. And anyway, why would he bother? Did he really think she was that much of a threat?

Maybe he'd lured her away from her apartment because he wanted to search it again. But if so, what was he looking for? More information about his exoneration?

Her brain cataloged more scenarios, but none of them made sense. She sighed, irritated. She'd have to revert back to her original plan.

She left the coffee shop and entered Campbell's address into her GPS system. When she got to Campbell's house, she didn't see a red Ford Focus anywhere, on this street or down a side street. The front yard had a bare spot where a car had sat.

She looked around. Most of the shotgun houses had shades or curtains covering their windows. The street was deserted, except for a group of teenaged boys who looked bored and itching for something to do—preferably something exciting and maybe illegal. As she watched, one of them made a gesture and they took off down a side street.

Clutching her purse closely, Rachel got out of her car and locked it. As she walked down the cracked sidewalk to Rick Campbell's front door, she caught a whiff of onions on the breeze. From somewhere, a woman yelled for her children to *get back here right now. Supper's on.*

Rachel walked up the two steps to the door and knocked, but the door swung open. She hadn't noticed that it was unlatched, because the house behind the door was dark.

"Hello?" she announced timidly. Then, "Hello?" a little louder.

Nothing. The house felt empty, but she didn't want to go inside without knowing for sure. "Rick?" she called, loud enough that she was sure anyone in the house could hear it. "Rick Campbell?"

She waited for a minute, counting off the seconds, then spoke again. When the house remained silent, she glanced up and down the street and at the neighbors' houses, making sure there was still no one outside, then she pulled her Glock from her purse, hoisted her now much lighter bag over her left shoulder and held the gun in her right hand, supported by her left.

"I'm coming in," she stated, then shouldered the door open. The house was as dark as it had seemed from outside. She noticed a faint odd smell—metallic and slightly sweet. She reached out and felt along the wall for the light switch. When her fingers touched it, she flipped it on.

The room was nearly empty. A threadbare couch sat on the scratched hardwood floor. A cardboard box served as a coffee table. Rachel led with her weapon, hugging the outside wall as she crept toward the kitchen. The living room and what little she could see of the hall were empty.

She angled around the door to the kitchen, weapon first. She stuck her head out and around, taking a snapshot of the room with her brain, then ducked back. Closing her eyes, she called up the scene. Sink piled high with dishes, trash can overflowing with Styrofoam boxes and fast-food cups. Newspapers scattered across a card table. But no sign of Campbell.

She crossed the kitchen to the hall. The sweetish, metallic smell was stronger there, and it turned her stomach. She took deep breaths, hoping to stave off nausea as she checked the front bedroom. Nothing in there but a mattress on the floor and a blanket that looked like it had been jerked off the mattress and tossed aside. The second bedroom was empty.

At the end of the hall was a door. Had to be the bathroom. She reluctantly shouldered the door open, dreading what she was about to see.

She stared in horror at the scene before her. The pink bathtub was streaked with red. It was blood. Diluted blood. There was a ring of it around the drain. Drops and dribbles stained the hexagonal floor tiles and led toward the door.

She turned around and looked down the hall. The droplets continued down the hall, smeared slightly where she'd walked, although the blood was mostly dried.

She should have seen the drops. She should have recognized the smell. God knew she'd encountered it often enough in her forensics training. She closed her eyes and saw the faint stars that often preceded a fainting spell. She took deep breaths but of course they didn't help, they just filled her head with more blood scent.

She clamped her hand over her mouth, waiting for the acrid saliva that presaged her throwing up. She wished she had menthol rub to dab under her nose, but she hadn't expected to walk into a crime scene.

Crime scene. Adrenaline shot through her like a blast of cold air. She was standing in the middle of a crime scene.

A crime scene with no body.

She stood still, her finger on the trigger of the Glock. She knew what she was supposed to do. She should already have called 9–1–1, but there was no body to go with the blood, and she had no good reason to explain why she was there.

Maybe she should call Ash. He'd know the best thing to do. Rachel dug her phone out of her purse as a vision of what would soon happen whirled in her head. The room would be crawling with police officers, detectives and crime scene experts, and she'd be carted off to an interrogation room.

She shook her head, and then immediately regretted it when the stars she saw increased in number—by millions. She crouched down, hoping to ward off the fainting spell.

She hit the speed dial for Ash without really thinking about it. When he answered, she found herself at a loss for words for a split second.

"Rach? What is it? You okay?" he said when she didn't speak.

"Yeah. I—uh—" She swallowed and shifted her weight as she sat back on her heels. "I'm at Rick Campbell's house."

"What? Are you all right?" he blurted. "Rach?"

"I'm fine, Ash, but—"

"What the hell are you doing there?"

"Ash, please! Listen to me. Campbell's not here but there's blood all over the bathroom, and—" She stopped. She hadn't looked closely at the living room floor. There were probably drops of blood there, too.

"Blood? Rach—get out! He could be there!"

"He's not. His car's not here—"

"Damn it. Have you called 9–1–1?"

"No, I—"

"Why not? Why're you calling me?"

"I don't know. I just hit your number."

She heard the whoosh of his breath. She could picture the exasperation on his face. "I'll call them. What's the address?"

She had to stop and think before she could recite it.

"Don't talk to anybody until I get there," he commanded.

Chapter Twelve

When Ash got to the address Rachel had given him, there were three police cars with lights flashing, and three other vehicles besides Rachel's parked near the house. He wove his way through curious onlookers and parked on a nearby side street, then loped back to the house. When he got to the door, a couple of uniformed officers were coming out.

"What's going on?" he asked them, flashing his detective's badge.

"Apparently that hot DNA specialist found the door open and a bunch of blood," one of them said, jerking his thumb backward.

Ash had to restrain himself from grabbing the officer's collar and reminding him that Rachel Stevens was a Ph.D. and senior to him. It didn't really matter right now. Right now he had to see if she was all right.

"Where are you going?"

"Detective Chasen told us to canvass the neighbors."

Ash nodded. Once he knew Rachel was all right, he was going to lay into her good for pulling this ridiculous stunt. He couldn't believe she'd even thought about talking to Campbell alone. He pushed past the officers and opened the front door.

There was a crime scene investigator in the living room,

shining an ultraviolet light on the floor and marking each spot. She looked up. Ash flashed his badge.

The CSI pointed behind her. "The bathroom," she said. "Watch my markers. Best way might be through the kitchen."

He could hear the low roar of people talking as he wove his way carefully past her and through the kitchen.

The scene that greeted him in the hallway looked like chaos—just like every crime scene he'd ever walked in on. Back when he was a rookie, it had taken a little while for him to figure out that what looked like utter confusion was actually a very odd but efficient meld of tasks, all of which were priority number one.

He glanced into the front bedroom and saw Neil Chasen talking to Rachel. He'd leave them alone for now, because he wanted to see the bathroom.

He was glad Neil was here. He'd been the detective on Rachel's home invasion, so she'd be comfortable with him. He was an excellent detective and a natural leader, so Ash knew that he'd have the scene walked off, cataloged, photographed and sealed as soon as was humanly possible. Meanwhile Ash knew better than to get in his way.

Two more officers were standing in the bathroom door. As Ash walked up, one said, "I guess we'd better get going. We've got a lot of hospitals to check."

Ash stood aside and let them pass. Inside the bathroom, a second crime scene investigator was making a digital recording of the room. When he stepped inside, the CSI glanced up. Ash showed him his badge, and he went back to his camera.

The walls of the bathtub were streaked with blood and the floor had a pink film all over it, with a ring of darker pink around the drain.

What the hell had happened here? It looked like the

scene of a suicide, but suicides didn't disappear from the scene.

Suddenly, a shard of fear ripped through his chest. He took out his phone with a trembling hand and dialed the mansion. His aunt answered.

"Aunt Angie. Where's Uncle Craig?"

"He's watching TV. I'll take him the phone."

Ash felt relief loosen his constricted chest. "No, that's okay. Don't bother him." But he wasn't done being worried. "Have you seen Natalie this afternoon?" He hoped he sounded casual.

"Yes. She ate dinner with us. Ash, what's going on?"

So much for sounding casual. "Nothing. I've just been wondering how everybody's doing. When did you last talk to Devin?"

"Not today. I wish you'd get over here more often. I miss seeing you."

"I'll definitely get by there this weekend or next, okay? I've just got a heavy caseload right now."

"I know you do, dear. Are you working on your parents' case?"

He looked around. "Yeah, I am. I'll see you soon, okay?"

"All right. Please be careful."

Ash hung up. He had one more phone call to make. He dialed Devin's cell. After a couple of rings, his older brother answered. Again, relief flooded Ash's chest. "Hey, Dev, what's going on?"

"What's wrong, Ash?" Devin said sharply.

Ash cleared his throat. He must sound terrible, the way everybody was reacting to his questions. "Nothing," he answered. "Just checking to see what you're up to."

"Right. Now, what the hell's the matter with you?"

"I'm standing in Rick Campbell's bathroom." He could

tell Devin things that he'd never tell Aunt Angie or Natalie. "The tub's covered in blood and he and his car are gone."

"What? What happened?"

"No idea, but we're working on it. I called Aunt Angie. I was afraid—"

"Uncle Craig might have snapped?"

"Yeah."

"And now you're calling me? Well, thanks for including me in your short list of suspects."

"Hey. I was worried about you."

"Yeah, I know. Thanks."

"Later," Ash said and hung up. He walked down the hall, avoiding the markers, and stepped into the bedroom where Neil and Rachel were talking. Rachel saw him and her fearful, pinched expression softened. She started toward him, then checked herself.

Neil followed her gaze. "Kendall. Dr. Stevens was just telling me that you were her first call. What time was that?"

Rachel's head whipped around. "I told you, it was—"

Neil held up his hand. "Hold on now, Rachel. This is protocol. Let Ash answer for himself."

She nodded. "Sorry," she muttered.

"I can tell you right here," Ash said, pulling out his cell phone. "She called me at eleven minutes after seven. As soon as we hung up, I called 9–1–1. The 9–1–1 call can't be more than one minute later."

Neil consulted a previous page of his notebook. "That's just about right. What did she say to you?"

"I'm sure she's already told you."

"I shouldn't have to remind you that these questions are routine, Detective."

Ash nodded. As much as he hated it, Rachel had involved him in this crime by calling him, so he had to cooperate. "I believe I said *Rachel, what's wrong?* Then she said she'd found Campbell's front door open and blood all over the bathroom. I asked if she'd called 9–1–1 and she said no. So I told her I would, and I told her to get out of the house and lock herself in her car. Not that she listened to me." He glared at her.

Neil looked at Ash, then Rachel, then back to Ash. He wrote very deliberately for a few seconds.

"Dr. Stevens. Why didn't you wait in the car?"

She shook her head.

"What did you do between calling Detective Kendall and when the police arrived?"

"I crouched on the floor, looking at the pool of blood," she said tiredly.

"Did you talk to anyone?"

"No. Not until the two uniformed officers came in. I told them what I'd told Ash, that I had found the front door open and the blood covering the bathroom floor."

"I think we probably need to go to the station. I've got some more questions for you, and we need to get out of CSI's way anyway."

"You're taking her in?" Ash asked.

"Just so I can find out everything she knows about what happened here."

"What makes you think she knows anything?"

Neil squinted at Ash, then took out his cell phone and punched a number. "Joe, leave Mason to finish the canvassing. I want you to take Dr. Stevens to the station in her car. Find a room where she'll be comfortable and get her whatever she wants to eat and drink. I'll be there soon."

He hung up and looked at Rachel. "He'll be here in a minute. Let's go outside onto the porch." He placed a hand in the middle of her back.

Ash followed them out to the front porch where the

officer was waiting. He took over for Chasen and guided her down the steps to her car.

She looked at Ash. He nodded reassuringly. Then he turned to Neil. "I heard an officer saying they were checking the hospitals. Are you treating it as an attempted suicide?"

"I'm not treating it as anything. I'm trying to cover all the bases."

"Including that Rachel sneaked in here, killed Campbell, set it up as a suicide and carted off his body?"

"Don't be an ass," Neil snapped.

"Well, don't treat her like a suspect."

"I'm not. I'm treating her like a material witness."

"We both know what that means," Ash retorted. "You don't seriously think she's involved in this, do you?"

"No," Neil said. "Not by herself."

"What the hell's that supposed to mean?" Ash asked. "Are you suggesting that I—"

"You and your family have a lot of reasons to resent Campbell."

"No, we don't," Ash said firmly. "He's been cleared of the murder. We have no feelings toward him except maybe to feel sorry for him for having served twenty years for a crime he didn't commit."

"That's how you view him? As a victim?"

Ash's ears were burning, he was so angry. "Of course. My family didn't convict him, but we were glad he was locked up. Now that he's been proven innocent, of course we're glad he's free."

"You know I'm going to have to talk to them, don't you?"

"Ah, hell, Neil. They're going through so much right now."

The older detective shrugged. "You know it has to be

done. I wouldn't be doing my job if I didn't record their whereabouts when this happened."

"Well, leave my sister out of it. She couldn't possibly have done it."

"Ash, I understand what you're saying, but you know I can't do that."

Ash cursed and pushed his fingers through his hair. "Have your CSIs found anything to suggest that any of my family was here?"

"I can't answer that." Neil appraised him. "What was Rachel doing here?" he asked.

"Hell if I know. The first I knew of her even thinking about Campbell was when she called me earlier."

"What do you think she wanted with him?"

Ash shook his head. "You're not luring me into that spiderweb. She'd have to answer that question herself."

"Yeah." Neil looked at his watch. "I need to get back there and get started."

"How long are you going to keep her?"

"Depends. Why?"

"I'm not letting her go home alone tonight. I could sit in on the interview with you."

"Nice try, Detective," Neil said wryly. "You can catch up on your paperwork or something until I'm finished with her."

"Thanks for the suggestion, but I think I'll observe."

"Suit yourself." He turned and called out to CSIs. "I'm heading out. Get me your reports ASAP. This is going to play really badly on the news."

Ash got in his car and headed over to the station house, thinking about what Neil had said. He was right. This *was* going to be a media circus. Once the press found out that Rick Campbell, falsely imprisoned for twenty years, had disappeared and blood had been found in his house, they were going to come after the Kendall family with a vengeance. By tomorrow morning they'd be swarming the mansion like angry hornets.

But that was probably nothing compared to what the police would do. The task force was already working on reopening the Christmas Eve Murders case. Now they'd focus on his entire family, questioning them about their whereabouts at the time of Campbell's murder, probing into their private lives, hounding them and treating them like suspects.

He blew out a frustrated breath and picked up his phone. He needed to warn everybody so they wouldn't be blind-sided this time.

"THAT'S NOT AN ACCEPTABLE answer," Detective Neil Chasen said as he paced back and forth behind the straight-backed chair Rachel was sitting in.

"Well, I'm sorry, Neil, it's the only answer I've got," Rachel retorted, rubbing her temples with her fingertips. Her head was beginning to hurt and little stars twinkled at the edge of her vision.

"Let's try this again," Neil said. "You went outside to sit on Ash's porch because you couldn't sleep."

She sighed. "That's right. It was dark, sometime in the early morning hours. I may have been out there a half hour when a car turned onto the street and cut its headlights. It drove around the cul-de-sac and stopped in front of Ash's house. I guess it must have stayed there with its engine idling for about three hours. I didn't want the driver to see me, so I didn't move but eventually dozed off on the glider. The sky was beginning to lighten when a change in the engine noise woke me up, and I got a look at the license plate."

"So then you went inside."

"Right." She nodded and immediately regretted it. "Neil, I've got a headache. I wasn't hungry earlier but now I need something to eat, or at least something to drink. Not coffee. I missed dinner."

Neil looked up at the one-way mirror and nodded. Rachel knew all about the one-way mirrors in the interrogation rooms. She'd even stood behind them listening to interrogations a few times. But she'd never been on this side, with a detective standing over her.

"All right. You'll have something in a few minutes. Now tell me exactly what you did when you went back inside. Why did you leave Ash asleep on the couch? Why didn't you wake him and tell him about the car?"

She rubbed her temples again. "Could we skip all that and go directly to the answer you think is unacceptable?"

"Sure. We can do that. As long as this time your answer's not *because he called me.*"

She shrugged. "But that is why."

Neil rolled his eyes. "Come on, Rachel. You told me you'd had the license plate run, and gotten his address. You'd already decided to talk to him, and I want to know why. *That's* the answer that doesn't work for me."

"I don't have a good answer for that," she said, spreading her hands. "When I found out it was Campbell's car parked in front of Ash's house, it worried me. I was afraid he might be planning to do something to Ash."

"That brings us back to my previous question. You didn't bother to tell Ash, a police detective who deals with that type of thing on a daily basis. Instead you decided to take your dad's service weapon and go to Campbell's house alone. Why didn't you wake Ash?"

Rachel arched her neck and grimaced at the tightness. "All right, all right." She didn't want to go into all the reasons she'd done what she'd done, mostly because she really didn't know exactly what they were.

"Of course it would have made more sense to let Ash know that Campbell was watching his house and let him handle it." She sighed. But she'd wanted to give him something—to solve something for him—so he would have one less thing to worry about instead of one more. If she told Neil that, she'd have to tell him what else was weighing on Ash's mind. She'd have to tell him she was pregnant.

"Ash was upset with me for—for several reasons. And Campbell going free is really wearing on him and his family. I wanted to take care of one problem for him."

Neil's brows shot upward. *"Take care of?"*

"Oh, for crying out loud, Neil. You know what I mean," she snapped. The little stars behind her eyes were growing in number. Soon she'd have to lay her head down or risk fainting.

At that moment a knock sounded on the door. "Thank goodness," she murmured.

An officer brought in a wrapped vending machine sandwich and a lemon-lime soda. She tore into the sandwich, which was pimento cheese and surprisingly good, and gulped the soda.

"Could you just let me write all this out and sign it? I really need to get some sleep," she mumbled through a mouthful of sandwich. She swallowed, then looked up at Neil. "That's assuming you're not going to arrest me."

"You know how this works, Rachel. This interview is being recorded. It'll be transcribed and then you'll get to sign it."

"But the transcriptionists don't come in until eight o'clock. I can't stay here that long. Neil, please."

"You can go in just a few minutes. Tell me about the phone call from Rick Campbell."

Rachel devoured the last bites of the sandwich and washed it down with soda. Then she took a deep breath. She felt a lot better, and the stars were fading. "I got home from work yesterday, and took a nap. I was planning to go to his house around seven-thirty and ask him what he was doing sitting outside Ash's house. I have a carry permit," she added, as if that would give her more credibility. From the look on Neil's face, his attitude about her packing was exactly the same as Ash's.

Neil pulled out a chair and sat down. "So you told me."

"I'd just picked up my purse and keys when my house phone rang. It was Campbell. He said he wanted to ask me some questions. He wanted to meet me somewhere. He offered to come to my office or meet me in a public place. So I suggested The Whole Bean Thing the next day—today—but he never showed up."

"Was that the extent of your conversation?"

"No." She paused. "I asked him if he'd been watching Ash's house. I thought he was going to just hang up, but finally he admitted he had. He said he'd been following me. He'd wanted to talk to me, but Ash was always there." She looked at her hands. "He said he just wanted to be close to me."

Neil glanced up at the one-way mirror, then back at her. "Are you listening to yourself?" he asked. "Campbell was *stalking* you. And you went to his *house!*"

"Yes, I did, and it's a good thing, or you may not have discovered he was missing for days."

"So I guess it never occurred to you that he might have been luring you there to hurt you or kill you."

Chapter Thirteen

Ash met Rachel as she came out of the interrogation room.

"What are you doing here?" she asked.

"I waited for you. I didn't want you driving home alone tonight," he told her.

"You were watching me, weren't you? From behind that one-way mirror."

He nodded. "We need to talk."

She held up her hand. "Not tonight. I'm going home."

He caught her arm. "No, you're not. At least not alone. If you won't come to my house, I'll spend the night at your apartment."

She looked at him in surprise, and he knew why. He'd never stayed over at her apartment while they were dating. That was one of the methods he'd developed over his years of casual dating. He made it a practice never to spend the night with a woman. His theory was that if he never brought them to his house or woke up in their beds, their attitude would remain casual, like his. It usually worked.

"You never have before. Why you think you need to do it now?"

"Because Campbell could be out there somewhere. Neil was right. He could mean you harm."

"Oh, come on. Nobody walks away after losing that much blood."

"*If* it's his blood."

Rachel's green-gold eyes widened and her hand went to her temple. "Wow. I can't believe I never thought of that. I guess I'm more tired than I thought I was." She bit her lip. "Whose blood do you think it is?" she asked.

Ash shrugged as he stepped in front of her to open the door leading to the parking garage elevator. He pressed the button and the car came right away. "I have no idea, but it's much more likely that he killed someone there and drove away with the body than that someone killed him and then drove him away in his own car."

They got on the elevator and he punched the number three button.

"My car's on four."

"I'll drive. We'll get your car tomorrow." He braced himself for more arguing, but she nodded, apparently too tired to object.

Rachel was silent on the ride home. That was okay with Ash. He needed to process what had happened. The first thing that had popped into his head when he'd seen the blood in the bathtub and dripped onto the floor was that Uncle Craig had gone off the deep end and managed to find out where Campbell lived.

His fingers tightened on the steering wheel as he sent a prayer of thanks skyward that his family were all accounted for. That the blood in Campbell's bathroom wasn't Kendall blood.

But whose blood was it? Campbell had been incarcerated for twenty years. He'd been free for less than a week. He'd apparently never been anything but a small-time burglar. How had he ended up with someone's life-blood spilled in his house? And where was he?

Ash pulled into his driveway and cut the engine. He got

out of the car and waited for Rachel to exit on the other side. She did, but then stopped before she closed the door.

"I don't have any clothes," she said.

"You can wear that tomorrow," he responded impatiently. "Who's going to notice?"

She threw up her hands in a helpless gesture. "Fine. You can take me by my apartment in the morning."

"Fine," he responded.

Once they were inside, Rachel breathed a sigh of relief. She crossed the living room into the kitchen and opened the refrigerator. She stood there looking inside.

"You hungry?" Ash asked as his gaze took in her subtle curves and the way she stood, one hip cocked, as she inventoried his fridge. He thought only men did that—stood in front of an open refrigerator door. But he had to admit, he liked the view.

"That sandwich was okay, but yeah, I'm hungry."

"There's cheese in there."

"Do you have crackers?"

"I'm pretty sure I do. But I can fix you something." He walked to the cabinet and opened it. "Something from a can. Soup? Or chili?"

She made a face. "I'd rather have the crackers."

On the top shelf, out of her reach but easily within his, was a box of wheat crackers. He grabbed them. They were unopened, which was probably good. That meant they weren't too old.

Rachel found the individually wrapped American cheese slices in the back of the refrigerator and took one. She set the food on the table and went back to the fridge and got the grape juice.

Ash got himself a beer and sat down at the table with her. He dug out a handful of crackers from the box.

Rachel unwrapped the slice of cheese and tore bits of it to eat with the crackers. "What time is it?" she asked.

"Almost eleven."

"I'm going to be so tired tomorrow."

"At least you won't have to go to work," he commented.

"What? Tomorrow's Saturday?" She shook her head. "I lost track of what day it was."

Ash studied her as she finished the last bite of cheese. She started to get up but he put a hand on her arm. "Wait," he said. "I need to know something."

"Ash, I'm really tired and I have got to take a shower."

"What were you doing, going after Campbell like that?"

She gave him a quick look, then lowered her eyes to the box of crackers. She took a cracker out and broke it in half, then broke one of the pieces in half. "I couldn't sleep the other night, after we—you know. Plus I was too warm, so I went out onto the porch and sat."

Ash did know. He'd fallen asleep on the couch with her in his arms after they'd made love. He couldn't believe he hadn't woken up when she got up. But then, he'd been drained, physically and emotionally, first from immersing himself in the case files of his parents' murder, then from the unexpected and amazing sex.

He pushed the memories of her lush, sexy body and the way they'd come together so easily out of his brain so he could concentrate on what she said. "You saw the car, too," he said, watching her reaction.

Her head jerked up and her oddly colored eyes stared at him. "You knew about the car?"

"I saw it a couple of nights earlier, but I couldn't get its license plate. Red Ford Focus?"

She nodded. "I have a friend in the DMV," she said. "It belongs to Campbell's mother."

"Damn it, Rach. Why didn't you tell me? I can't believe

you just went running off over there. You could have been hurt or killed." He blew out a breath in exasperation. The more he was around her the more he saw her stubborn side. "And I can't believe you thought it was a good idea to take your gun."

"I didn't go *running off over there,*" she retorted. "I thought about it. When my friend told me who the car was registered to, I thought about going to see Mrs. Campbell. But then I remembered I had an unsanitized copy of the DNA report that the commissioner's chief of staff gave me the day of the press conference. It had the address of the house Campbell was staying in. I *was* going to go see him but he called me first."

"Why didn't you tell me?" he asked again. "I'd have gone with you."

"No, you wouldn't have. You'd have gone yourself, or just told me to forget it." She paused for a brief moment. "I wanted to find out why he was outside your house. I wanted to be able to bring you something—a solution instead of another problem. I thought it might make up for my part in setting him free. Plus I was afraid he was stalking you. But you heard what he told me on the phone. He wanted to talk to me. He was scared to death that you'd find a way to put him back in prison."

"I don't care what you found out from him. What you did was dangerous."

"I don't know about dangerous, Ash. He was very nice and apologetic on the phone."

"Not hard to fake."

"I don't think he was faking it."

"Did you tell anyone—?" Ash was interrupted by his phone. He'd set it on the table in the foyer as they'd come in. He retrieved it.

"Ash." It was Neil Chasen.

"Neil. What's up?"

"I need to speak to Rachel. I don't have her cell number in front of me. Didn't I understand you to say she'd be with you tonight?"

"Yeah, she's right here." He looked at her. "Anything new about Campbell?" he asked.

"We've got a BOLO out for him and his vehicle."

"No luck yet, eh? Well, maybe something will turn up tonight. Hang on," he said, turning to Rachel. "It's for you."

Rachel looked surprised, but she took the phone. "Hello?" she said tentatively, then, "Oh. Neil. Hi. Please don't tell me you have more questions for me tonight. I've got to get some sleep." Her left hand slid across her stomach and she spread her fingers protectively.

The gesture slammed Ash in the chest. He hadn't forgotten that she was pregnant, but he tended to forget how much it affected everything she did, until he saw her sliding her palm across her nearly flat tummy, or she'd get woozy and pale.

Then Neil said something and she squeezed her eyes shut. He couldn't tell if she was relieved or upset.

"Okay, sure," she sighed. "What time?" She listened for a moment. "Could we make it nine?"

Ash pointed to his phone and to himself.

"Okay," she said again, then, "Ash wants to talk with—" She paused. "Someone to run the DNA? Sure. I can call around and see if I can get someone to come in."

Ash frowned and gestured for the phone again. She handed it to him. "What's going on, Neil?"

"I need the DNA on that blood run tomorrow."

"What did the chief say?"

"I haven't talked to him yet," Neil replied.

"Oh." Ash was surprised. Neil was definitely a by-

the-book detective. Ash found it odd that he hadn't consulted Hammond, but then, it was almost midnight on a
Friday night. "What did CSI come up with? Anything?"

"The blood is O positive, which matches Campbell—"

"And what? Eighty percent of the population?" Ash put
in.

"Right, and it had been there at least twenty-four hours.
That's why I need the DNA analyzed ASAP. If the DNA
matches—" He stopped.

"Yeah," Ash said, filling in what Neil didn't say. "The
press is going to declare open season on the police department, the Campbells and my family."

"You'd better be prepared," Neil warned. "They're already out in force. They know Campbell's missing. So far
we've kept the info on the bloody bathroom away from
them, but it's only a matter of time."

Ash grimaced. Before all this was over, his family could
be destroyed—again.

IT TOOK RACHEL SEVERAL phone calls before she found a
forensic technician who was willing to come in on Saturday without a guarantee of pay.

"You owe me lattes for a month," Debra Jensen had told
her.

"Double lattes," Rachel had agreed.

Neil had refused to allow Rachel to be involved in the
testing. He'd secured her promise to stay at Ash's house
while Debra ran the blood evidence.

Rachel and Debra had talked about how to conduct
the analysis so that there would be no chance of missing
a second person's blood in the mix. Rachel had recom-
mended twenty-five random samples be run from various
areas in the pool of blood. Debra agreed. Rachel and Ash
paced Ash's living room as they waited to hear the results.

When Neil finally called them, Rachel listened to his excited chatter for a few seconds, then demanded to talk to Debra.

"Be careful, Rach," Ash said. He was standing next to her, doing his best to hear both sides of the conversation. "You don't want to have any questions come up about the results."

"Neil, didn't you get the okay from Uncle Charlie?" Rachel asked.

"Uncle Charlie—" Neil echoed.

"Sorry. Chief Hammond. He and my dad were big fishing buddies back in the day."

"Oh." Neil paused for a fraction of a second. "I couldn't get in touch with him. I talked to his daughter this morning. She said Thursday night he was talking about taking a long weekend to go fishing, but he complained that he might be getting a bug. So she made him soup and told him to stay home and turn off his phones."

"That's probably what he did," Rachel said. "But I'll bet he's at the cabin today, bug or not. Especially with this beautiful weather. He loves to fish as much as my dad did."

"That must be it," Neil said. "Because his cell phone's turned off or out of juice."

"Who's next in line when the chief's out?"

Beside her, Ash uttered a laugh. "Neil."

"Not only that," Neil put in. "I got a call this morning from the head of the Christmas Eve Murders Task Force. He told me they're officially reopening the case and appointing me lead detective."

"Okay, then, Lead Detective," Rachel said, "let me talk to Debra."

As soon as Debra said hello, Rachel asked her, "What have you got?"

"A very interesting result," Debra said.

Rachel groaned. "Don't be coy. You're killing me. Did you get a match?"

Debra laughed. "I took the twenty-five samples and printed transparencies. Neil stacked them one at a time on the light table—"

"And they all matched!" Rachel heard Neil shout. "You should have seen them. Twenty-five sheets that lined up perfectly."

"Twenty-five samples—twenty-five matches," Debra added.

Then Neil was on the phone. "That means all the blood was from one person, right?" he asked.

"Yes, it does," Rachel said, feeling triumphant.

Beside her, Ash touched her arm. She glanced at him. "You know whose blood it is, don't you?" he said. "I can tell by the look on her face."

How did he do that? How could he just look at her and know what she was thinking?

"What?" Neil said. "What did Kendall say?"

"Rachel knows whose blood it is," Ash said.

"I don't *know*," she corrected. "I wish I could see the pattern. But I've got an educated guess."

"Well, let's find out. Debra, can you compare the results?" Neil asked.

Rachel heard Debra's footsteps on the tile floor of the lab.

"Debra's comparing the results with the blind sample I ran two weeks ago," she said to Ash.

She held her breath, waiting, but it was only a couple of seconds before Neil said, "Ha!"

"Neil?" she prompted.

"It's his. It's Campbell's," Neil said.

"So Campbell's was the only blood at the scene?" Ash asked.

Neil relayed the question to Debra, then said, "Debra says yes."

"Of course that brings up the obvious question," Rachel said. "Where is Campbell, and is he alive or dead?"

"If Campbell was killed there in his bathroom," Neil said, "another question remains, who took his body and his car?"

Ash nodded, although only Rachel could see him. "That is the sixty-four-thousand-dollar question," he said into the phone. He looked at his watch. "I'd like to talk more about this, but it's after five and Rachel needs to eat. I say we meet somewhere. Rach, are you *craving* anything in particular?"

"Craving?" Neil's surprised voice came through the phone.

Ash cleared his throat, trying to think of what to say. He'd spoken without thinking, now he had to somehow backtrack. "Low blood sugar," he said, sending her an apologetic look.

"Right," she agreed. "Low blood sugar."

"I see," Neil said noncommittally.

THE THREE OF THEM MET UP at a local restaurant. Ash and Neil got steaks and Rachel ordered sea scallops and polenta. By silent mutual agreement they waited until after they ate to talk about the case.

"Get this," Neil said. "You saw all the marks in the hall and the living room. They're vertical drops. There are a lot of them, but not as many as there ought to be if someone climbed out of the bathtub wet and bloody."

"And there were no bloody footprints, either," Rachel added.

"Except for yours."

She grimaced. "I know. I accidentally smeared some of the blood drops in the hall."

Neil continued. "I think if Campbell had walked out of the house under his own steam, we'd see his footprints and a whole lot more drops and smears of bloody water."

"What are you saying?" Ash asked.

"CSI thinks someone carried him out," Neil said. "Probably wrapped in something. Campbell was—is scrawny. He's around five feet six inches, and probably not a hundred thirty pounds soaking wet. It wouldn't be hard for a decent-size man to carry him."

"You think it was one person?"

"Don't know."

"What about trace? Anything that could have come from the killer?" Rachel asked.

"Nothing yet. There were fibers from a cotton sheet on the mattress and quilt but no sheets, and the quilt looked like it had been tossed in a corner. I'm guessing the sheets were what he was carried out in."

"What happened with the hospitals?" Ash asked.

"Nothing. My officers finished with them early this morning." Neil sighed. "They talked to the neighbors, too, who weren't real happy about being questioned. One guy was outside smoking and saw a car pull up, but he didn't pay any attention to the make and model. When he went to work the next morning, the car was there but Campbell's wasn't. I'm afraid we may have to abandon the idea of attempted suicide and a helpful neighbor taking him to the hospital."

"So you're left with murder," Ash said.

Neil nodded, looking at his watch. "Looks like it." He pushed back from the table. "I need to go. I've got an early morning tomorrow. I've got to talk to your family."

"On Sunday? Give me a break, Chasen." Ash threw out a hand, palm up. "Give *them* a break."

"I ought to be interviewing them tonight, but I'm too tired to think, and I doubt they'll make a run for it between now and tomorrow."

"Thanks for the vote of confidence," Ash said wryly. "I'll see you at the mansion tomorrow."

"Come on, Kendall, how long are you going to dog my tail?"

"Until you figure out that nobody in my family murdered Rick Campbell."

Chapter Fourteen

"Why in hell can't they leave us alone?" Craig Kendall barked Sunday morning. He was holding a mug of coffee and pacing back and forth, stopping every couple of steps to glare out the window at the press vehicles parked on the other side of the gate.

Ash clenched his jaw. His uncle's anger coupled with his loud mouth was going to antagonize Neil. Luckily, he didn't have to warn him. Aunt Angie was already taking care of that.

"Craig, please don't throw a tantrum. Fred, tell him. We need to cooperate. We know we didn't do anything wrong."

Fred Farley, the family's lawyer, opened his mouth, but closed it again when Craig shot him a narrow glance.

"Ash, dear, what kind of questions will he ask?" She twisted a dish towel in her hands.

Before Ash could answer, Craig pointed out the window. "Somebody just opened the gate!" he shouted. "What the hell?"

"It's okay. I gave Neil the gate code." As Ash spoke, his cell phone rang. It was Neil, his voice pitched high with excitement. "Kendall, we got a call about a body in Horseshoe Lake," he said.

Ash's heart rate skyrocketed, zero to sixty in two seconds. "Hold on," he said, turning the phone away from his family and walking through the dining room into the living room. "Okay. Horseshoe Lake? That's what—thirty miles from here?"

"More like forty. The local uniforms pulled him out. An ambulance is bringing him here."

"So you're not at the lake? Who just came through the gate here?"

"That's Detective Jones. He'll be doing the interview."

"So where are you?"

"I'm with the M.E., waiting for the body. His height and weight are consistent with Campbell's."

"Any sign of the car?"

"The deputy chief out there tells me that one of his officers took his boat out. He radioed back that he saw a car in the lake. It's going to take them a while to pull it out."

"I want to see the body."

"Kendall, there are so many conflicts of interest—"

"I'll see you there," Ash interrupted and hung up. He walked back to his aunt and uncle, who both looked at him with apprehension plain on their faces.

"Detective Chasen can't be here himself to interview you." Down the hall a loud bell chimed over his last word. "That's Detective Jones. He'll be asking you questions. Remember what I said. Just tell the truth."

Ash kissed his aunt's forehead. "Turn that frown upside down," he teased with a smile. "That's what you used to tell us."

She slapped playfully at his arm as her lips turned up in a small smile. "Go on. Shoo."

Ash drove straight to the autopsy lab. When he got there, Neil and the M.E. were standing over the table where the corpse lay. He was dressed in a shirt and pants. He wasn't in too bad a shape, considering where he'd been, but his skin was a grayish-white, as if there was no blood under it.

No blood. Ash's gaze snapped to the swollen wrists. There was a deep gash running vertically up the arm from the pulse point. The suicide attempt?

"Damn," he said. "What happened to his face?"

"Probably catfish," the M.E. said. "Noses, lips and ears usually go first, along with fingers and toes."

"That's not going to make it easy to ID him, is it?"

Suddenly, anger welled up in him so sharp and hot that it cut off his breathing for an instant. It had been building ever since Chief Hammond had told him Campbell was going free. He clenched his fists and tried to banish the urge to rush to the table and beat the corpse to a pulp for getting itself murdered.

He forced himself to listen to the M.E.

"From the condition of the body, I'd say he's been in the water forty-eight hours at least," the medical examiner was saying. "I'll need a water sample from the lake and its ambient temperature before I can be more specific."

Neil barely glanced at Ash. The M.E. didn't even look up. "What about height and weight?" he asked the doctor.

"Height's easy," the M.E. replied, pressing a remote controller in his hand to activate the tape recorder. "This is a rather poorly nourished white male in mid-to-late-fifties. He's approximately five feet six inches and looks like he may have weighed somewhere in the range of one-twenty to one-thirty." He punched the button again.

Ash's anger flared again. "That's Campbell all right," he said sharply. "What about C.O.D?"

At that question, the M.E. looked up, an amused expression on his lined face. "This is as far as we've gotten."

Ash pointed to the wrists. "Look there. Maybe he did commit suicide."

Neil looked at the gashes. "Dr. Patel, what do you think?" he asked.

The medical examiner looked at the wrists through a lighted magnifying glass. "Well, there do appear to be hesitation wounds. That's normal in suicides. But to be positive, I'll need to examine him more closely."

"So the hesitation wounds prove that Campbell did commit suicide?"

"I wouldn't go that far. I need to complete the autopsy first."

While they were talking, Ash was examining the rest of the body. "It doesn't make sense that Campbell would commit suicide. Why now, when he's free for the first time in twenty years?"

"Are you asking me?" Patel asked.

"Sure, if you've got an answer."

"I've been Medical Examiner here for seventeen years. People have odd reactions to getting out of prison, especially after an extended period of time. Some are agoraphobic. They find themselves a small apartment or room—an enclosed space—and refuse to leave it."

"You've seen a released prisoner kill himself?" Neil asked.

The M.E. nodded. "Two cases that I remember."

"Why?"

"You'd have to sit down with a psychiatrist to figure out the answer to that question. All I can tell you is that it happens."

Ash looked at Campbell more closely. "What's this, on his head?" he pointed out.

"Let me see," Patel said.

Neil stepped over beside Ash to watch as Patel turned Campbell's head and examined his scalp. "There's a contusion here. Again, I need to examine the wound more closely to give you a definitive answer, but it looks like a blow from a blunt instrument."

"Did it happen accidentally in the water, or did someone hit him?" Neil asked.

"I tell you what, gentlemen. Why don't you let me do the autopsy and send you my report. Then if you still have questions, I'll be happy to answer them, based on fact rather than conjecture."

"Thanks, Dr. Patel," Neil said. "I'll wait to hear from you."

As they left, Ash said, "It makes no sense that someone would hit Campbell and then put him in the tub to try and fake a suicide."

Neil stared at him. "You do realize you're not on this case, right?"

Ash shrugged. "You don't want me around, just say so."

Neil's jaw twitched. "I've allowed you to observe as a professional courtesy, but tomorrow when the chief gets back, I figure you and me both are going to get our butts chewed."

Ash grinned. "But that's tomorrow. Are you heading out to check on the car?"

"I am, but I suggest that you get home to your girlfriend. She might be craving pickles this morning."

"Ah, hell, Neil."

"Did you think I'd forget that comment about cravings? I've got three kids, remember?" Neil assessed him. "How did you, of all people, let that happen?"

"Carelessness," Ash said dully.

"Careless? Ashanova?" Neil stopped at his car and pressed the remote unlock. "I don't think so. Rachel's a beautiful woman, though I'm not sure you're good enough for her."

"I can't argue with that," Ash said ruefully. "But I'm not—"

Neil waited a beat. "You're not what? Not ready to settle down? You should have thought of that—when? She can't be too far along."

"About nine weeks, I think."

"You've got a lot going on right now."

Ash laughed. "You think?"

Ash swung by the mansion on his way back to his house. He found Angela, Craig, Natalie and Devin sitting at the kitchen table. None of them looked happy. Natalie was pale and the corners of her mouth were pinched and white.

"The questioning was rough?" he asked.

"Rough?" Uncle Craig barked. "That's what you call it? No, it wasn't rough. It was brutal, humiliating. How in hell can the police justify treating victims like suspects? No! Not even suspects—criminals!" He banged his palm on the kitchen table.

Natalie jumped and Angela uttered a little cry.

"Uncle Craig," Devin said. "You're upsetting Nat and Aunt Angie."

Spilling a mouthful of curse words, Craig pushed back from the table and got up. "It was the detective that upset everybody. And that wimp shyster Farley didn't open his mouth."

He glared at Ash. "What good is it having a cop in the family if you can't protect us from that kind of bullying?"

"Uncle Craig—" Ash started, but his uncle was past listening.

"I'm going out," he said bluntly and left the room.

Ash started after him, but his aunt caught his eye and shook her head. "Don't. You'll just get into a fight."

"Where's he going?" Ash asked.

"I don't know. He doesn't tell me." She looked down at her hands and back up to meet his gaze. "He wasn't—he's been out every night this past week—except Friday when you called."

"Out? Out where?" Ash looked at Devin, then at Natalie, but they shook their heads.

"He wouldn't say where he was—not even to the detective." Angela's eyes filled with tears and they overflowed onto her cheeks. She swiped at them, but they kept falling.

Ash felt a sense of dread weigh on his chest. "Are you saying he wasn't here Thursday night?"

"That's right, dear. He's been so upset ever since that Rick Campbell got out of jail."

"Oh, don't cry," Natalie said, her voice hoarse. "It'll be fine."

Devin pushed breath through his clenched teeth. "The guy had the tact of a bull elephant. Nat was white as a sheet by the time he finished with her."

"I hate that Neil had to turn the questioning over to somebody else. He'd have been much more considerate. And I'm sorry I wasn't here. I have news, though. They found Campbell's body."

"Body?" Angela echoed in a quavery voice. "Oh, dear."

"Where?" Devin asked.

Ash looked at Natalie, but she had her hand on Angela's arm and was comforting her. Worrying about their aunt seemed to help her. She was getting some color back into her cheeks.

"They found him in Horseshoe Lake. They found his car, too. He has deep cuts on his wrists, but he also has a wound on his head."

"What does that mean?" Devin asked.

"The M.E. will have to get back with us about the cause of death, but I don't think it's going to be ruled a suicide."

RACHEL WAS GOING STIR-CRAZY. Ash had left before eight to be with his family while Neil questioned them. She'd woken up when he had left, but then she'd gone back to sleep for another hour.

When she got up, she realized she was stranded. She'd let Ash talk her into leaving her car in the division parking lot and riding with him to dinner last night.

So she'd made coffee, realized it wasn't decaf and only allowed herself half a cup. She'd cleaned up the kitchen, stripped the beds, washed and dried the linens and then remade the beds. When she checked the time, it was barely two o'clock.

Frustrated, she'd sat down to watch an old movie. It ended exactly the same way it had the first time she'd seen it over twenty years before.

Sighing, she glanced at Ash's file box. TV or case files from The Christmas Eve Murders? It was no contest.

She turned off the TV and dug into the box. She'd seen quite a bit of its contents but certainly not all. Retrieving a pad and pen from her purse, she pulled a stack of files from the box.

When she heard Ash's key in the lock, she realized she'd been sitting there for over three hours.

Ash seemed a little surprised to see her. "Oh, hi," he said dully.

"Ash? Is something wrong?" Rachel set the files aside and stood. "How did the questioning go?"

He shrugged as he pulled his weapon from the paddle holster at the small of his back. He went into his bedroom and she heard him put the gun in his bedside table.

She went into the kitchen to get some water.

After a couple of minutes, he came in, opened the refrigerator and got himself a soda. He sat down at the kitchen table and popped the top, then stared at it. His whole demeanor was dejected. His shoulders slumped.

"Are you hungry?" she asked. "I could heat up some soup."

He shook his head and took a swig of soda.

She sat down across from him. Apprehension skittered through her. He'd been worried about how his uncle Craig had reacted to the news that Campbell was getting out of prison. "How did the interviews go? Did your uncle do okay?"

"Not very well," he said flatly, twirling the can to make little patterns in the condensation that ran down onto the tabletop. His mouth was thin and set. He looked exhausted, beaten down.

She reached out and touched his hand and he looked up at her. To her shock, she saw tears glistening in his eyes. Her face must have reflected her alarm, because he looked down again and shook his head.

She waited, afraid of what he was going to say. *Don't let any of his family be involved in Campbell's disappearance,* she prayed.

"You know, bad things happen to a lot of people," he said finally, still playing with the soda can. "When you're a cop, you see it every day. Most people seem to cope really well even with the worst tragedies. I thought I was."

Rachel wanted to reassure him, but he had something on his mind and she didn't want to interrupt him. He needed to talk. He'd told her himself that he'd never talked about his parents' murder.

"I guess I got the idea that life was too short. That I needed to get as much fun out of it as I possibly could." He stopped and cleared his throat. "For me fun equaled girls. I always liked girls."

Rachel smiled. *And girls like you.*

"The other side of me wanted to do something about people like Campbell—" He stopped and shook his head. "Like whoever killed my parents. I joined the army, but that didn't work. The reality of fighting other human beings is *way* different from the idea that I had. I was sent to Iraq. It was hot and dirty and boring, with a few bursts of absolute terror." He took another swallow of soda.

"After my tour was over, I went to the police academy. I didn't like killing. Plus, I wanted to stop the scumbags here at home. Taking murderers off the streets seemed like a noble profession." He shrugged. "That's worked out pretty well."

"You're very good at your job," Rachel said softly.

Ash met her eyes. "Yeah, I am. But it turns out that's not enough. I sure have screwed up my personal life."

His words stabbed her in the heart. Was he talking about the baby?

Ha, she answered herself. What kind of question is that? Look at him. He's *Ashanova,* and he was perfectly happy until she dropped that bomb on him.

"Ash, wait." She didn't want to ask the question, but she couldn't help herself. "Why do you think you've screwed up your personal life?"

"Why? Look what I've done. I've always prided myself on not hurting anyone. But I was careless and now you're pregnant."

"I'm *not* sorry about the baby," she said, her voice hitching.

He wiped his hand down his face. "Well, I am. I had no right to make love to you without using protection. It was irresponsible."

Her heart took another hit. "It takes two to make a baby, Ash. I'm very sorry that you regret what happened, but I don't."

"Damn it, Rach. You know I don't mean it like that."

"Oh? How do you mean it?"

He shook his head and a rueful smile curved his lips. "See? I can't open my mouth without saying the wrong thing." He stood and drained the soda can. "Chalk it up to a long, frustrating day."

He tossed the can into the trash, then headed to his bedroom and closed the door.

After a few minutes, she heard the pipes squeak and the water heater come on. He was taking a shower.

Sure enough, within twenty minutes he emerged, dressed in a new white T-shirt and old jeans. His hair was damp and he was freshly shaven. Just looking at him made her heart hurt. He looked like everything she'd ever wanted.

"Didn't you say something about dinner?" he asked. Then he smiled and her heart broke into a million pieces.

Dear God, let the baby look like him, she prayed. Because she was going to miss that smile.

BY THE TIME HE'D FINISHED showering, Ash felt a lot better. Of course he knew why he'd been so melancholy. He was terrified that Uncle Craig may have killed Rick Campbell.

A week ago, he'd have said his uncle couldn't have done something like that. But seeing his anger this morning and the information from Aunt Angie that he'd been gone every night—including Thursday—well, if he'd had to testify under oath, he wasn't sure he could say he was one-hundred-percent sure Craig wasn't capable of murder.

If his uncle had killed Campbell, that would be the last straw.

The fragile, precious bond that had held his family together would be broken and the thing he'd feared for twenty years would come to pass.

His family, his foundation, would be destroyed. He'd give anything to believe that Uncle Craig wasn't guilty, but he couldn't. Because he knew that anger. He recognized it. It burned inside him, too.

As Rachel served up the dinner she'd made, Ash told her about finding Campbell's body and his car in Horseshoe Lake. She asked a lot of questions. By the time he'd finished two helpings of her surprisingly good concoction of chili, vegetable soup and rice, and had given her the rundown of Dr. Patel's preliminary findings, his mood had improved a lot.

He helped Rachel with the dishes, then went into the living room. There were manila folders and papers scattered over the coffee table and the couch. "What's all this?" he asked her.

"Oh," she said. "I was going stir-crazy here all day, so I went through the case files and made notes."

Ash frowned at her. "Notes about what?"

She moved some stacks of papers to the coffee table from the couch, then picked up a pad and pen and sat down. "Listen to this," she said, looking down at the pad.

"I made a list of things that were never followed up. Number one, Campbell didn't have the ring or the gun. Two, the scratches on his arm were never positively matched to your mom's fingernails. Nor is there any mention of checking the windowsill that Campbell claimed scratched him. Three, Campbell swore he saw a man leaving the area of your parents' house, and there's no follow-up on that. From what I can tell, no one ever even interviewed another suspect."

Ash thought back on the telephone conversation he'd overheard in Chief Hammond's office. "It does seem odd that the chief didn't check out those discrepancies. He reamed somebody for not doing a thorough canvass of a neighborhood in a murder case just the other day. He said he hated shoddy work. But then when I asked him about the ring and the gun and the second man, he nearly reamed *me*."

"Your parents' case was twenty years ago," Rachel said. "Still, it's not like Uncle Charlie was a rookie. He started around the same time as my dad did, so that would mean he'd had almost ten years' experience by then."

"Yeah." He gestured toward the box. "There was nothing in there about the windowsill?"

"There's a photo of it, marked with a number but nothing other than Uncle Charlie's handwritten notes."

"And the man Campbell saw running from the scene?"

She shook her head. "Same. Nothing but his notes. And there's no mention of anyone canvassing *your* neighborhood," Rachel said. "Now, *that's* careless. Twenty years later, there's probably no chance of finding a soul who remembers seeing the man," Rachel said. "Even if they remembered, they probably couldn't describe him."

Ash vaulted up off the couch. "Damn it," he said, slamming a fist into his palm, his anger rekindling.

"Ash?" Rachel said, her voice tinged with worry.

He deliberately unclenched his fists and took a deep, cleansing breath.

"I'm okay," he said. "It's just that Campbell's the only one who saw anything that night. Now he's dead, and the answers to those questions died with him."

Chapter Fifteen

Rachel yawned and covered her mouth.

Ash smiled at her. "Tired? I haven't asked you how you're feeling."

"Wow. Suddenly I'm sleepy," she said as she stood. "I'm feeling good. I don't seem to be getting nauseated as much, but I'm trying to be careful what I eat."

She started toward the guest bedroom. "I guess I'll go to bed." She paused. "Are you all right?"

He nodded, standing and following her. "When's your next doctor's appointment?"

She turned at the guest bedroom door and smiled, thinking about what the doctor had told her. "In about three weeks. I'll be getting an ultrasound."

"An ultrasound?" he asked, his features lightening. "To look at the baby?"

Seeing his expression, Rachel felt, for the first time, that she wasn't facing this long, unfamiliar road alone. His face was filled with curiosity and concern, he hovered over her protectively and his eyes held a soft glow she'd never seen before.

"Will we find out if it's—if he's—" he took a deep breath "—a boy or a girl?"

She chuckled to hear him stumbling over what to call

the baby. "It's pretty early," she said as her hand moved to her tummy.

Ash's eyes widened. "Early? So we won't—?"

"Apparently, he or she is going to look more like a peanut than anything else. We may have to wait another month or so to find out what we have."

He looked down at her hand. "Can you feel the baby?"

"Not yet. Mostly I feel a little achy in my lower back and my clothes aren't fitting like they should."

He looked at her, his eyes softer than she'd ever seen them before. "Can I touch you?" he asked tentatively, holding out his hand.

"Sure," she said, not sure at all. He put his hand over hers where it rested on her belly. It was large and warm and encompassed her hand completely. Slowly, she slid her hand out and placed it on top of his.

"Your belly is rounder."

"A little," she replied softly as the warmth of his hand seeped through her clothes. From deep inside her came a glimmer of desire. She held her breath. If he moved at all, she was afraid that the desire she was holding in check might flare. And he was too close to her. There was no way he wouldn't feel it. She struggled to keep her attention on their conversation and off her swirling hormones. "The doctor said because I'm small, I'll start showing sooner."

"What about having the baby? Will you be okay?"

"He said my hips were good and wide," she said wryly.

"That's a good thing," he whispered.

She lifted her head slightly. "What?"

But instead of repeating what he'd said, Ash leaned down and touched his lips to hers. He whispered something, his mouth moving against hers, tickling her skin, then he kissed her.

Sure enough, her yearning flared and heat spread

through every cell in her body, pulsing and flowing like lifeblood, all the way to her fingers and toes. She rose on tiptoes and kissed him back, wanting him more at this moment than she ever had before. And that was a lot.

"You're so beautiful," he whispered, putting both hands on her waist. "So lush and sexy."

He deepened his kiss, his tongue exploring the inside of her mouth and teasing and sparring with hers. Her body softened, opened to him, ready for him. But her brain wouldn't surrender.

Then his hands slid up her waist to her breasts and he moaned as he cupped them.

"You are such a turn-on," he muttered, his mouth leaving hers and sliding down to her neck. Then his hands encircled her waist and lifted her.

"No," she whispered, but he held on to her and lowered her until he could reach her lips.

She almost surrendered, almost wrapped her legs around him and let him take her to his bed, but one word he'd uttered kept echoing in her ears.

Lush. He was turned on by the changes in her body caused by her pregnancy.

"Ash?" she murmured.

He made a sound deep in his throat and moved one hand to cup her bottom, urging her leg to bend.

"Ash," she said more firmly.

He looked at her, his eyes soft with passion. Then he lowered her until her feet touched the floor. "Did I hurt you?" he asked.

She shook her head. "Why are you doing this?"

He blinked. "Doing what?"

"This." She spread her hands. "Coming on to me like this? What's it about?"

"About?" He looked bewildered. "It's about—"

She waited, but he seemed stuck there. And that was the problem, she realized. He was stuck—stuck in his own casual *love 'em and leave 'em—happy* world. She supposed she could understand why he'd grown up determined to squeeze as much fun as he could get out of life.

But that didn't work for her. It never had. She'd started dating him because of his charm and good looks. She'd continued because she'd fallen in love with him. For him the fun was the point. For her it was merely lagniappe.

"I'm sorry, Ash. I can't do this." She stepped backward. "Just take me to get my car so I can go home."

He scowled at her. "It's after ten o'clock. We're both going into the office tomorrow. There's no reason to get out tonight. You're tired."

She opened her mouth to protest but he cut her off with a wave of his hand.

"I promise I'll leave you alone." He nodded toward the guest room. "That door locks if you don't trust me." With that he turned on his heel and went into his bedroom and shut the door.

The sound of the latch was as loud as a prison gate slamming shut. Not locking her in. Locking her and her child out of Ash's life.

WHEN ASH GOT TO WORK the next morning—a Monday— Neil was in Chief Hammond's office. Tamping down the urge to barge in and find out what was going on, Ash went straight to his desk. He had reports to write on some cases and a court appearance to prepare for. He was happy to leave the explanations of everything that had gone on over the weekend to Neil.

But every few minutes, he glanced up to be sure Neil was still in there and willing him to come by his desk once they were done. He hoped Hammond didn't stop Neil from sharing information about Campbell's death with him.

When his phone rang, he actually hesitated before answering it. He didn't want to get involved with something and miss Neil.

Finally, he picked up the handset. "Detective Kendall," he said shortly.

The call was about an abandoned vehicle on the Martin Luther King Bridge at I-70. The vehicle's doors were locked and there was a wrapped bundle in the backseat that, according to the officer on the scene, could be a baby or a small child.

Ash had to pass Deputy Chief Hammond's office as he headed out. Neil was still in there. He was talking and Hammond was standing, his arms folded and a pensive look on his face.

It wasn't until after five when Ash got back to his desk. By then most of the squad room was empty. Hammond's office was dark. Ash dialed Neil and heard his phone ringing from across the large room.

He headed toward the sound, hanging up as he stepped into the tiny break room where Neil was digging his phone out of his pocket with his left hand while he poured coffee with his right.

"Hey," Ash said. "Any left?"

Neil held up the pot. Ash grabbed a mug, checked to see that it was relatively clean and held it out so Neil could pour him a cup of coffee. Ash drank a swallow and grimaced.

Neil chuckled as he leaned against the counter and sipped from his cup. "Ever notice how everybody drinks the coffee and then they make that same face?"

Ash nodded. "I had to go out before you got through with Hammond. What's up with him?" he asked.

"It was like his daughter said. He woke up with a bug on Thursday," Neil said. "He took her advice that evening and turned off his phone and holed up on the couch that Friday, sleeping and watching football all weekend. He called his boss, but nobody let us know."

"So how's he doing?"

"He said he was okay this morning, but he didn't look real good. He was pale. Really kind of green. When I came back by his office around three, he was gone."

"What'd he say about Campbell?" Ash asked.

"He was surprised—but he believes Campbell killed himself—out of guilt."

"What?" Ash poured the last half of the coffee down the sink and rinsed his cup. "How did he figure the car and the body got to the lake?"

Neil shrugged. "His theory is someone found him— maybe his mom or his brother—or both of them—and they managed to haul the body off."

"I guess," Ash commented. "Have you questioned them?"

"Yeah. They're pretty torn up. Claim they don't believe he'd kill himself. His mother said he had a job interview on that Friday." Neil looked at Ash. "Detective Jones said your uncle wouldn't answer any questions about his whereabouts this past week. Apparently, he wasn't home on Thursday evening."

Ash sighed. "Are you going to bring him in?" he asked harshly.

"I need to know where he was on Thursday night."

Ash blew out a frustrated breath between his teeth. "Go easy. He's hanging on by a thread."

"Jones said he acted belligerent, but he looked terrified."

"I know," Ash said. "I'm afraid he's going to have some kind of breakdown."

Neil eyed him narrowly. "You don't look so good yourself. Do you think your uncle could have killed Campbell?"

Ash couldn't answer. He swallowed against a lump in his throat.

Neil didn't say anything for a moment, then to Ash's relief, he changed the subject. "I've got the M.E.'s full report."

Ash cleared his throat. "What did he say about the blow to the head?"

"He couldn't verify whether the blow to Campbell's head was pre- or post-mortem. He said the fish did a number on the wound."

"What about cause of death?"

"He said the cause of death was exsanguination. He said being in the water all that time made it hard to pinpoint the time, but taking everything into consideration, he figured Campbell died late Thursday night or early Friday morning."

"What did CSI find on the car?"

"Oh, get this. There was almost no evidence in the car. They found a few traces of blood, all Campbell's. But almost everything, including hairs, fibers and fingerprints were obliterated by the water and the mud. They did turn up a few partial prints."

"Yeah?"

"None of them are clear enough to make an ID. In fact, they're so degraded that when the lab ran them, they came up with too many matches."

"How can you have too many matches?"

"Okay, here's what the fingerprint tech told me. Fingerprints aren't as unique as people once thought they were. We all have certain things in common. He said the smaller the section of print he has, the more matches he gets from the database."

Ash looked at his fingertips. "Okay. I think I get it."

"Well, from Campbell's car, he got—" Neil paused and pulled a folded piece of paper from his breast pocket "—four partials that yielded twenty-three hits." Neil spread the sheet open on the counter, inviting Ash to look at it with him.

"That's one of the partials," he said, pointing. "And this graph indicates the points of similarity."

Ash couldn't make much sense out of what he was looking at. "What? They're ID'd only by social security number?"

Neil folded the sheet of paper and took out his notebook. "He sent me his report online. I've given printouts to a few officers to run down the people. I told them to work on the ones located closest to St. Louis first. But listen to this. These are just a few of the twenty-three hits." Neil met Ash's gaze. "This is going to blow you away."

Ash folded his arms. "Okay. Blow me away."

Neil started reading. "Among the four prints, there are matches to Campbell, of course, his brother and his mother, an embezzler serving time in Ohio, a postal worker in Florida—"

"So far I'm not blown away. Are you going to read me all of them?"

Neil continued as though Ash hadn't interrupted. "A judge, three men serving in the military, a shoplifter *and*—" He looked up at Ash expectantly.

Ash waited, holding his breath. Whatever Neil was onto, he was certainly excited about it.

"Two people connected to Campbell's case. A guard at the prison where Campbell served his time, and the chief."

Ash thought he'd missed something. "The chief what?"

"Our chief. Hammond."

"Son of a bitch," Ash said, at a loss for words. "Did you tell him?"

Neil nodded. "That's one of the things we were talking about in his office. He thinks it's funny—ironic, you know."

"Funny? What are you going to do?"

"He's already given me a report on his whereabouts Thursday night. He said he was feeling bad, so he called his daughter, who brought him over some soup. They watched part of a ball game together, then he went to bed early."

"What do you think?"

"What do you mean, what do I think?" Neil answered. "I think I've got twenty-three possible suspects and I've got to talk to every single one of them." He took a deep breath.

"I spent this morning talking to Campbell's mother and brother. Both of them deny everything, of course. Campbell's car belongs to his mom, so naturally their fingerprints would be in it. Oh, and they're alibiing each other."

"How far have the officers gotten contacting the others?"

"I've heard back on three. The prison guard was on duty Thursday night until eleven. He went home and was there all night, according to him and his wife." Neil flipped another page. "A medical student at Washington University couldn't be reached. His mother told my officer he took off a semester and is spending it with his dad in Chicago."

Ash pushed his fingers through his hair. "So you've got five likely suspects, including the Deputy Chief of the Ninth Division of the SLMPD, and none of them have airtight alibis."

Neil's frustration was showing. He closed the notepad and jammed it into his pocket. "That's right. And unless one of them decides to confess, I don't have squat. They all had the means, they all had the opportunity and not a one of them had a motive."

Chapter Sixteen

Rachel got home before six. When she unlocked the door to her apartment, she saw her suitcase sitting in the middle of the living room. She hadn't taken time to unpack before everything had happened with Rick Campbell.

She sighed and dragged the case into the bedroom, set it in the corner and tossed her purse onto the bed, its heft reminding her that she'd meant to put her gun back in the trunk of her car. She didn't like carrying a loaded weapon around.

But she was too tired to go back outside now. Too tired and too upset. She was angry at Ash for telling her all about his doubts and fears, and then trying to play on her sympathy by coming on to her. And she was angry at herself for almost giving in.

He'd looked right at her and told her that he'd screwed up his personal life. Well, guess what? He'd screwed up hers, as well.

She'd been perfectly happy, with a great career and plenty of time to think about marriage and family. But then he'd made her fall in love with him. Worse, they'd been careless, and now she was pregnant. Pregnant with no strings attached.

The problem was she wanted strings. No. Not strings. *Rings.* She wanted Ash in her life, in her baby's life.

She wanted him to love her, and that was never going to happen.

She pressed her lips together and blinked against the stinging in her eyes as she changed into fleece pajamas. As she came out of the bedroom, thinking about what she wanted for dinner, there was a rapping on her front door. She went into the living room and peered through the peephole.

It was Deputy Chief Hammond. She was a little surprised. Uncle Charlie had never shown up at her apartment before. In fact, since her dad had died, they'd spoken at work, but that was all.

She opened the door. "Uncle Charlie, hi. What are you doing here?"

"Can I come in?" he asked, looking ill at ease.

"Sure. Come on in," she said, stepping aside to let him pass. "I heard you were sick. Are you feeling better now?"

He didn't answer her question, he just walked into her living room and looked around. "Nice place. It's kind of small, but it looks comfortable."

"It is," she said, watching him curiously. A faint uneasiness began to quiver inside her. There was something wrong about him showing up here.

"What can I do for you?" she asked. "Would you like something to drink?"

He shook his head, still looking around the room, as if he wasn't sure how he got here. Rachel watched him apprehensively.

Finally he sat on the edge of her couch and turned his attention to her. She perched on the arm of her easy chair. For some reason, she was reluctant to sit.

"You've turned out awfully pretty, Rachel," he said.

"Thank you," she said, pasting a smile on her face.

"Your dad was always so proud of you." Hammond

leaned back. "He used to say there wasn't anything you couldn't do."

Rachel laughed a little uneasily. "Well, he was my daddy. That's what daddies are supposed to say."

"Nope," Hammond said. "That wasn't just a father talking about his daughter. He really believed it. I believe it, too. You can do anything."

Rachel studied him closely, still unable to figure out what was going on with him. He was pale, except for dark splotches of red in his cheeks, and his hands were trembling. She didn't smell liquor, but she supposed there were drinks, like vodka, that didn't give off telltale odors.

"For instance, you did a great job on the DNA for the Christmas Eve Murders." His tone changed, hardened.

The uneasiness in her chest grew to fear and slithered up her spine. "Uncle Charlie?" she started.

He held up a hand. "But you've got to go back. Go back and tell the truth. Tell them that the sample was contaminated. That you were wrong. The DNA did belong to Rick Campbell."

"But it didn't, Uncle Charlie. The report I turned in was absolutely right. The tests were conclusive. I'm sorry."

Sweat had popped out on his forehead and was pooling and running down his face and neck.

"You're not feeling well," she said, standing. "I heard you had a virus. I'll get you some medicine." Her phone was in the kitchen. Maybe she could call Ash or Neil. She was afraid he was delusional. Maybe he was still feverish from the virus.

"Sit down, Rachel," he said.

When she turned back to look at him, she saw that he was holding a Sig Sauer pointed at her.

"Uncle Charlie!"

"Sit down!" he bellowed suddenly, pushing himself to his feet. "Sit! Right there!"

She sat. "Uncle Charlie, I don't understand. What's wrong?"

"I'm disappointed in you. Your daddy would be disappointed, too. You let that preppy A.D.A. Meeks sweet-talk you. I don't think you'd alter the sample." He took a shaky breath. "I know you. I've known you since you were a baby. You're not like that. But you don't know much about men. What did you do? Let Meeks into your lab late at night? Let him touch you? Get you all hot and bothered so that when he disappeared for a few minutes after you two had—you know—you didn't pay any attention to what he was doing?"

Rachel stared at him in shock. "No!" she cried. "Tim Meeks? I *never* let him touch me. He was never in the lab. I don't know what you're talking about."

Hammond stood and paced, waving the gun. "You don't? Well, let me fill you in. Meeks and that D.A., Allen, made a big mistake, digging into the Christmas Eve Murders. That case was closed. Everything was fine. Until they got you to run that analysis. I'm telling you, Rachel, you were duped. Somehow, they changed the evidence to prove that the man I put in prison twenty years ago was innocent."

THERE WAS A KNOCK ON THE open door to the break room. Ash looked up and saw the night maid.

"Excuse me," she said. "Is it okay to clean now?"

"Sure," Ash said. "Come on, Neil. Walk back to my desk with me. Are you about ready to go?"

"Yeah."

"So how can you be sure none of your five suspects has a motive?"

"Look at them. What's Campbell's mother's motive? Or his brother's?"

Ash sat down behind his desk and intertwined his fingers behind his head. "Maybe they always had trouble with him. Maybe he was forever mooching money or getting in trouble, and their lives were much easier with him in prison."

Neil shook his head. "How about the prison guard?"

"That one's easy," Ash said. "Maybe Campbell had something on him." He paused. "And as far as the medical student is concerned, I have no idea why he'd have a beef with Campbell, but it'd be interesting to see what he claims his alibi is. It's not *that* far to Chicago."

"Okay, you're on such a roll, what about the chief?"

Ash looked at Neil, then off into the distance while he thought. Then he sat up. "Try this," he said, not exactly sure where he was going with the idea that had just popped into his head. "Hammond got his promotion because of the Christmas Eve Murders. Solving that case established his reputation. Once Rachel's DNA analysis proved that Campbell couldn't have committed the murders, Hammond ended up with egg on his face."

"Why should he care? He's the deputy chief. Nothing can touch him."

"Yes, it can," Ash countered. "Public opinion can."

Neil started to shake his head again, but instead he just stared at Ash. After a few thoughtful seconds, he said with an uncomfortable chuckle, "Okay. Let's say the chief killed Campbell. What the hell happened at Campbell's house?"

Ash raised his brows. "Seriously? You want to keep going with this?" Neil didn't move, so Ash went on. "Okay, then. The chief goes to Campbell's house, thinking he can overpower him and make it look like Campbell committed suicide. But Campbell fights back and Hammond has to hit him. Now the chief is panicking. He still tries to stage it as a suicide but realizes it's not going to work, so the chief carries Campbell out to Campbell's own car and dumps him and the car in the lake. Then he makes his way back to Campbell's house and drives his car home and pretends to be sick over an extended weekend." By the time Ash finished, he was out of breath and out of ideas. He spread his hands.

"Sounds impossible, I know," he said.

But Neil was staring at a spot somewhere behind Ash's head. "No," he said pensively. "No. Not impossible. But how does he get back to Campbell's house? It's nearly forty miles from the lake."

Ash shrugged. "Cab? Bus? Friend?"

"Not friend. I don't know about buses." Neil ran a hand over his buzz-cut hair. "As much as the cop shows would like us to think every cab and bus driver remembers every person they pick up, it isn't that easy."

"I know. We could go through all the cab companies' records, but that could take weeks, and what would we have? A fare that fits into the geography and the time frame. It's still no proof."

"I know."

Neil's voice sounded distracted. Ash frowned. "What is it?" he asked.

When Neil looked at him, Ash was shocked at the look in the other man's eyes.

"Oh, no," he said. "Tell me you're not thinking about bringing the chief in. He'll eat you for breakfast and not even belch."

Neil rubbed his eyes. "I've got to go through every one of the suspects the same way, but stick with me on Hammond for a minute. He takes a cab or a bus or some combination back to Campbell's house. He needs to clean up the bathroom. He knows forensics. All he needs to do is wash the blood down the bathtub drain, mop up the drips and footprints, and wipe everything down to get rid of his fingerprints."

"Right. Campbell and his car are gone. There's no sign of a struggle. We might take a look around, but we'd have no reason to mount a murder investigation. Campbell would go on the books as a missing person." Ash drummed his fingers on his desk. "So why didn't he?"

"When he gets back, somebody's outside smoking or just hanging around. Or a cop car drives by. The chief can't afford to be seen, so he gets out of there."

Ash tried to find holes in Neil's reasoning. There were a few, but they were small. "It's possible," he said.

"So now," Neil continued. "Say you're the chief, and you know we've found the body and the car, and some of the fingerprints were partial matches for yours, what would you do?"

Ash shook his head. "Okay, first of all, it would depend on whether I'd killed him or not," he said wryly, checking his watch. "Damn it, it's after eight. I need to check on Rachel." He pulled out his phone and called her but there was no answer. He tried her home phone, but voice mail picked up. He disconnected without leaving a message.

"I can't reach her," he said as worry twined around his spine.

"She's probably asleep," Neil suggested.

"She'd have her phone by her bed. She's had a couple of spells of light-headedness. She could have passed out." He looked at his phone. "Maybe I should call her mother and see if she's talked to her."

"Try Rachel's phone one more time," Neil said, "before you go off half-cocked and scare her mother to death."

RACHEL STARTED TO STAND. That was the second time her phone had rung. Hammond acted as if he hadn't heard anything, but as soon as she moved, he stopped pacing and pointed the gun directly at her chest.

"Don't move," he said.

"That's my phone. It could be my mother or—or Ash. If I don't answer they'll be worried and probably come over here to check on me."

Hammond smiled. "I don't think so. I'll bet you told Kendall you were going to bed early. He won't be checking on you. Now, we need to figure out how you're going to retract your findings on the DNA analysis for the Christmas Eve Murders."

"Uncle Charlie, I can't. Even if I tried, they've already got my results. The test speaks for itself. All the commissioner would have to do is have the tests run again by another lab, and they'd come up with the same findings."

"They'd have to get the DNA from your lab, right? You have access."

Rachel stared at him. "Yes, but all samples are kept under lock and key, and anyone who goes into the evidence cabinet has to sign the log. You know that."

"What if you don't sign it?"

"I have to."

"What if you don't?" he demanded through clenched teeth. "What would happen?"

Rachel didn't know how to answer him. Of course, the cabinet had a lock on it and everyone who opened it signed a book indicating the time open and the time closed, what their business in the cabinet was and documentation of anything they removed or added. But there was no electronic monitoring of the cabinet doors. Maybe he didn't know that.

"There would be an electronic record of the cabinet

being opened without proper signature and documenta-tion," she said. "The next time someone went to the cabi-net, they'd notice, and there would be an investigation." She wondered if the tremor in her voice had given her away.

Hammond sat still, watching her for almost a minute. "Where's the information recorded?"

Rachel forced herself to hold his gaze. He was trying to trip her up. "It's in—it's located in the—"

"You're lying, Rachel. Your daddy would be disap-pointed in you. There's no monitor on that cabinet." He gestured with his gun.

"Get up. We're going down to the lab and you're going to contaminate the remaining DNA from the Christmas Eve Murders."

"I can't do that."

"What if I told you I'd kill you if you don't?"

She shook her head. "You won't kill me. You can't. My dad was your best friend. You've been to our house. You know my mother." She hated that she sounded like she was on the verge of hysteria, even if it was true.

"Here's what I know. My career is going down the toilet if I don't do something."

"You don't know that. No one is going to blame you. Didn't you tell me there was a lot of public pressure back then to convict someone?" Rachel was talking as fast as she could, trying to remember everything she'd heard and read about the case. "And you had a strong circumstantial case." She gave him a quavery smile. "You'll be fine."

"That shows how naive you are, Rachel. The D.A. has his own stable of fair-haired boys, just waiting to take over my job and a lot of others. Allen's doing his best to get us—the old guard—out of the way. Nope. The only way I can save face is to discredit Allen. Once the commissioner finds out the DNA was contaminated so that it wouldn't match Campbell's, it'll be Jesse Allen's butt in hot water."

"But it wasn't contaminated."

Hammond stood and pointed the gun down at her. "Yes—it—was! You've got to accept that. There's no other explanation. Campbell was guilty. He was guilty as sin and nothing you or anybody else says is going to change that." He squinted at her. "Now get up!"

Rachel stood, holding her hands out at her sides. "I'm in my pajamas. I need to change," she said, trying for as much innocence as she could put into her voice. She needed to get into her bedroom and get her gun from her purse. It terrified her to go up against the chief, but she was afraid it was her only chance of surviving.

"Nope. No time. You'll go like you are."

Rachel tried to think, to plan. Once they got to the lab and she switched Campbell's DNA with someone else's, her "Uncle Charlie" would kill her. "I need to get my purse."

"Quit stalling. Walk to the front door and out."

"What about my keys?" she asked desperately.

"We're going in my car. You'll drive."

"But—I need them for the lab."

"Don't mess with me, Rachel. I know the lab door locks are electronic."

She was defeated. She had no idea what she could do to stop him or save herself. He probably had eighty pounds on her. And although she'd always thought of him as old, like her dad, he was only in his early fifties. She couldn't overpower him. She probably couldn't outrun him.

She knew she couldn't outrun his bullet.

"Uncle Charlie," she said, her voice breaking. "I'm pregnant."

He stared at her. "You're—"

She nodded as her eyes filled with tears. "Think about it. Dad would have the grandson he always wanted."

"It's a boy?" Hammond asked, his gun hand wavering slightly. "You know it's a boy? Who's the father?"

"Ash. He's so excited." Tears streamed down Rachel's cheeks as she told the half lie. The baby was Ash's, but he wasn't excited about it.

Hammond shook his head. "I'm sorry. I'm sorry, Rachel. But I've got to do this. You understand, right?"

"No, I don't. If you'd just leave it alone, nobody would blame you. You'd still be division chief. You'd still have your career."

Now sweat was streaming down the chief's face and soaking into the collar of his shirt. His skin had gone from merely pale to a sick greenish color, and the red spots in his cheeks were gone. "Stop talking, Rachel. Let's go. We need to get this done."

Rachel wanted to try one more time. She wanted to ask him to let her go to the bathroom, but he was barely holding on to control. She could tell it in his white-knuckled grip on the gun, the wild look in his eyes, the sweat pouring off his pale shocky skin.

So she walked toward the door.

"Go!" he shouted. "Get a move on."

"I'm scared, Uncle Charlie," she cried, letting the tears flow freely. She'd run out of ideas.

"Open the door," he ordered. "Now walk outside casually, like we're going out to dinner or something. If you try to run, I'll shoot you." He dug the barrel of the gun into the small of her back. "Do you believe me?"

She nodded. She could barely see for the tears glazing her eyes. She turned the doorknob.

"Hold it! We're going to walk down the sidewalk to my car. It's parked to the right in the first row. Don't stop for anything. If you see anyone you know, you smile, but that's all. No conversation. Got it?"

"I've got it," she said dully, and turned the knob.

The breezeway was well lighted, as was the sidewalk leading out to the parking lot. They didn't run into any of her neighbors, for which Rachel felt relieved. She had no idea how she'd have acted, and if she'd said or done the wrong thing, she might've gotten someone shot.

Hammond's gun in her back urged her forward. Rachel heard a car turn in, its tires squealing. She looked in that direction.

"Watch it, Rachel. Just keep walking. Ignore the hot rod." Hammond prodded her again. "We're going to my car. It's the black SUV over there."

She blinked tears away and tried to spot the vehicle he was talking about.

"Just keep walking straight until you pass between these two cars directly in front of you, then turn right. Go around the SUV and get into the driver's seat."

She was past the point of arguing with him. Because she didn't have her purse, she didn't have her driver's license, but she was going to be driving the Deputy Chief of the Ninth Division of the St. Louis Metropolitan Police Department. Even if someone stopped them, all they'd do was apologize to the chief and wave them on.

The tears kept falling. She wanted to touch her stomach, spread her fingers protectively over the precious place where her baby was growing, but she didn't dare.

I'm sorry, she said silently to her baby, holding her breath to keep from sobbing. She wasn't going to make it through this night alive, and her baby—Ash's baby—was going to die with her.

Chapter Seventeen

Ash killed the engine and jumped out of his car. He started to call out to Rachel and whoever was walking with her. All he could tell was that it was a male, and both of them were walking stiffly. Stiffly and doggedly. A flutter of apprehension in his chest told him there was something wrong.

He paused while there was still a row of cars between them. He wanted to get a better look at the man who was walking behind her.

At that moment they walked under a streetlight and he saw the features of the man. It was the chief. The flutter in his chest turned to full-blown panic. Without moving, he reached into his pants pocket for his cell phone and pressed the quick-dial button for Neil Chasen.

He slowly raised the phone until it was close to his mouth. "Neil, I need backup at Rachel's apartment. The chief's got Rachel. Repeat—need backup."

Before he finished speaking, Hammond muttered something to Rachel and they both stopped. Hammond swept the parking lot with his gaze.

He'd heard him, Ash realized in dismay. Still, he froze in place. If he stood as still as a statue, maybe the chief wouldn't see him in the dark. Once Hammond walked past the first row of cars, Ash could get the drop on him.

Hammond nudged Rachel with his hidden hand, and she started walking again.

Ash caught a reflection of light on metal. Damn it, Hammond had a gun on her back. His heart sank to his toes. No wonder they were both moving so stiffly. Within a matter of a split second, Ash's mind sorted through the possible scenarios for how this situation could play out. He didn't like any of them. The problem was, as soon as he moved, Hammond would see him, and a gun in a paddle holster behind Ash's back was no match for a gun that was already in Hammond's hand.

If Hammond squeezed the trigger in surprise, Rachel would be dead. Rachel and their baby. *Their baby.* Dangerous, hazy tears stung Ash's eyes. He blinked furiously. No time for emotion. He needed strength, courage and focus.

They were getting closer. Hammond had already heard him. Now he was alert to the sounds in the parking lot, waiting to see what had made the sound he'd heard.

So Ash decided to play dumb. He dropped his phone to the ground and muttered a curse as he bent to pick it up.

"Hold it," he heard Hammond say softly. "Stay still."

Ash straightened up. "Oh, hey," he said and stepped out of the shadows. "Chief. Rachel. What are you two doing? Going for a late dinner?"

He met Rachel's terrified gaze and tried, without showing any change in expression, to tell her telepathically that everything was going to be all right.

If he read her right, she knew he was lying.

Then he turned his gaze to Chief Hammond, who looked like hell. "Hi, Chief. I hope you're feeling better."

Hammond appeared to be stunned. His eyes darted from Ash to the right and back again. Ash figured he was measuring the distance to his vehicle and comparing it with the distance between Ash and them.

Ash held up his cell phone with his left hand. "I was trying to call you, Rach. I dropped my damn phone." He blew on the case, as if dislodging dust. "I hope I didn't break it." All the while he was talking and gesturing with his left hand, he was carefully and slowly inching his right hand back to grab his weapon.

"Ash," the chief said. "Don't move."

Ash froze. He stared at Hammond as if he couldn't believe what he'd said. He took a step forward. "Chief? What's the matter?"

Hammond wrapped his left forearm around Rachel's neck. She uttered a short, cut-off shriek.

Ash immediately raised his hands. He still held his cell phone in his left hand. "Chief? I don't understand—"

"Shut up!" the chief yelled. Pushing Rachel ahead of him, he moved forward, toward the end of the sidewalk and the beginning of the parking lot.

"Uncle Charlie—" she gasped.

"Shut up!" he bellowed. "Ash, get down on the ground. Flat, arms out to your side. Do it now!" He pushed Rachel farther forward, until they were nearly past the back ends of the cars. It gave Hammond a clear shot at Ash.

Ash knew if he sprawled on the ground, it would all be over. Whatever Hammond was planning, he didn't seem to care if he came out of it alive.

"Chief, listen to me. I know what happened. You went to Campbell's house, right? Was he already in the tub with his wrists cut?"

Hammond frowned. "How—?"

"I saw his bathroom. It's the only thing that makes sense. You got there too early. Bad luck. Ten more minutes and Campbell would have bled out and you could have left the scene and let someone else find him."

"Stop talking and get on the ground."

"Campbell's death would have taken the heat off the police department and you never would have had to defend your decisions."

"I made the right decision! Campbell was guilty!" Rachel winced and cried out as Hammond shoved the gun even harder into her back.

Hammond was running out of patience and Ash was running out of time "Chief, wait. The M.E. can't say whether Campbell was dead or alive when he suffered that blow to his head. What if you found Campbell dead and decided to drive him up to that lake so his mother wouldn't know—?"

"Stop it. Just stop it! Get! Down! Or I swear I'll shoot her." He dug the barrel of the gun deeper into Rachel's back. She cried out in pain.

Ash knew he would. He could see it in his pale, panicked face. He measured the distance between them. At least twelve feet. Too far. A standing jump would never carry him far enough to grab Hammond. But he was pretty sure of one thing. If he dived at him, the chief's response would likely be to push Rachel aside and turn the gun on Ash.

Ash could die. But by the time Hammond shot him, maybe Rachel could recover her footing and run. Or maybe Neil would show with backup.

He looked at Rachel, the woman who'd screwed up his carefree life by getting pregnant. The woman he wanted to make a new life with, raise their child with, grow old with.

Did he rush Hammond and risk dying? It was the only thing he could do to save Rachel.

Hammond squeezed Rachel's neck tighter.

"I can't—breathe," she gasped, grabbing his forearm with her hands and trying to pull. "Please—Uncle Char—I—"

"Shut up!" the chief yelled.

Ash jumped. He sailed toward the chief, knowing as soon as his feet left the ground that he was going to fall short.

Hammond let go of Rachel, who went sprawling to the ground with a scream, and turned his powerful Sig Sauer on Ash.

As his forward motion decayed and he began falling toward the ground, Ash's super-attenuated senses saw Hammond's finger squeeze the trigger, saw the powder flare, watched the bullet fly toward him.

The impact of the bullet propelled him backward. His fingers brushed Hammond's pant legs below the knee and Ash grasped at his legs.

He slammed to the ground, which hurt more than he'd ever dreamed anything could, and Hammond fell on top of him. Dimly, Ash heard the clatter of metal on pavement and something or someone screeching in his ears.

"I DO NOT—NEED TO GO to the hospital," Rachel protested through her sobs as she watched Ash's ominously still form being loaded into the back of an ambulance. "Please, let me go with him."

The EMT kept a firm hold on her arm and continued examining her neck. "He's in excellent hands. They'll take good care of him for you." He put his hand on the gun. "Now why don't you let me have this. You don't need it anymore. The policeman here wants to take it."

Rachel squeezed even tighter the handle of Chief Hammond's gun. She'd crawled across the pavement to grab it when Ash had knocked it out of his hand. If the sirens and the screeching of tires hadn't startled her, she'd have shot her "uncle." Because he had shot Ash.

The police officer stepped up and nodded at the EMT.

"Dr. Stevens, I'll take the gun now. We need to log it into evidence so we can prove whose it is."

Prove whose it is. She nodded and opened her fist. "Keep the chain of custody," she warned him, then sobbed again.

"Don't you worry. I'm definitely taking care of this weapon," the officer said solemnly.

The EMT pressed a place near her jaw.

She jumped.

"You've got some pretty nasty bruises here. Your neck is going to be real colorful for the next couple of weeks. Now, where else were you hurt?"

He'd already cleaned and put bandages on her elbow and her knees where she'd scraped them on the pavement.

"Uncle—Chief Hammond pushed the gun into my back. It—hurt." She squeezed her eyes shut. She knew she was acting like a baby, but she couldn't stop herself. She'd thought she was going to die. Then she'd watched Ash get shot. She didn't think she'd ever be able banish from her head the sight of his body jerking violently backward as the bullet slammed into him.

"What if he dies?" she whispered.

"The detective who was shot? I'm sure he'll pull through." *How* could he know?

"You don't know that!" she snapped. "Don't tell people things are going to be okay when you don't know."

The EMT had lifted her shirt and was looking at her back. "You've got some bruises here, too, but you should be fine."

She rested her hand on her stomach. "I'm pregnant," she cried, the sobs climbing up her throat again.

"Oh, yeah?" the EMT said. "How far along are you?"

"Nine weeks," she said as he felt her belly and took a stethoscope and listened.

"Congratulations. Looks to me like everything's fine. But we're going to send you to the hospital just to be sure."

"I told you—"

"No arguments," he said, crouching down so he could look her in the eye. She knew she had no choice.

TWO DAYS LATER, ASH WAS making his way slowly around the hospital room, collecting his belongings when a rap came on the door.

"Hey," Neil said as he walked inside, his gaze taking in the overnight bag and Ash's shirt and khaki pants. "What are you doing up? Didn't you just have surgery?"

"Two days ago." He gestured toward his left side. "Luckily Hammond was off balance. The bullet plowed a furrow in my side, but that's all." Ash reached across the foot of the bed for his shaving kit and groaned in pain.

"That's not what I heard. They told me that you were in surgery for two hours. That the bullet came way too close to your spine."

Ash shrugged and pretended to check the contents of his bag one more time. "So have you seen Rachel?" he asked casually.

"Not since that night. Her mom picked her up at the hospital and took her home with her, kicking and screaming."

Ash turned. "What does that mean?"

Neil smiled. "It means Rachel wouldn't leave until you were safely out of surgery and in the recovery room."

"Really?" Ash heard the longing in his own voice and cleared his throat.

"Really," Neil answered on a laugh. "You've got it bad, don't you?"

Ash looked back down at his bag and zipped it. "I don't know what you mean."

"Right."

"Did you come here just to give me a hard time? Because Nat's waiting downstairs."

"I just came from the chief's arraignment," Neil said, his voice sober now. "He pled guilty to murder in the first degree."

"What?" Ash was shocked. "Who the hell's his lawyer?"

"I don't know the guy, but he wasn't happy. He entered a plea of not guilty by reason of insanity and asked for a hearing to determine if the chief is competent to stand trial." Neil shook his head.

"Ash, you should have seen him. I swear he looks like he's lost twenty pounds and aged twenty years. He's not the same man. It's like the chief is gone and all that's left is the shell."

Ash sat down on the bed. "It doesn't make sense. What did he get out of killing Campbell? Except life in prison?"

"I think it was like you told me. He was going to try and make it look like suicide, but Campbell fought. After that, I think the chief just lost his mind and thought if he could make the body disappear—" Neil trailed off.

Ash shook his head. "I was making that up as I went along, hoping I could get him to let Rachel go. Did Hammond explain anything when he pled?"

"He talked, but he didn't make much sense. He just kept raving that Campbell had to be guilty. That he wasn't wrong twenty years ago and he wasn't wrong now. It was pretty sad to watch." Neil sighed. "He always seemed so—you know—large and in charge."

Ash laughed ruefully. "In charge, definitely." He stood again and gathered up his belongings. "Let's go. I'll walk down with you."

"Don't you have to wait for a nurse to wheel you down?"

"No. I already told them I was leaving under my own steam."

"What about flowers? You poor sucker. Didn't you get any flowers?"

"Nat already took them." He reached for the door and grunted.

Neil laughed. "How come she didn't take your bag?"

"Her hands were full."

"Give it to me." Neil took Ash's bag from him. "So you gonna let your aunt take care of you?" Neil asked as they reached the elevator.

"That would be great, for about twenty minutes. No, Natalie's taking me back to my house."

"So she'll be taking care of you."

Ash laughed weakly. The walk to the elevator had worn him out. He sucked in a deep breath. "That might work for an hour, but no. I'll be fine."

Neil assessed him. "Then you must feel a hell of a lot better than you look." When the elevator opened on the main floor, they walked out the doors together.

Neil waved at Natalie, who was leaning against her car, waiting. She waved back and gave him a smile, then she glared at Ash.

"Why aren't you in a wheelchair?" she scolded. "You look like you're about to faint."

"Give me a break, Nat. I'm fine."

"Yeah? Get in the car." She took his bag and held the passenger door open for him.

He sat carefully in the seat, then went to lift his leg. Pain grabbed his side and twisted like a giant fist. He gasped.

"See. That's what I thought. Lift your leg with your hand."

"With my hand? I'm not paralyzed."

"Do it."

Ash did what she'd said and found out it was much easier. "Okay, fine," he grunted, lifting the other leg and carefully positioning himself in the passenger seat.

Natalie grinned at him and slammed the door, then walked around to the driver's side and got in. "Where to, sir?"

"Home," Ash said, trying to figure out why his vision was going dark at the edges. He leaned his head back against the seat. "My house."

"Aunt Angie has chicken potpie cooking, especially for you."

"Please don't, Nat. I can't eat. All I want to do is sleep." He closed his eyes, but he could feel his sister's gaze on him.

"Okay, but you're the one who's going to have to tell her. I'm not about to try and convince her that you're better off home alone."

"No problem," Ash whispered, grimacing at the pain in his side. "Go by the drugstore first. I've got a prescription for pain meds."

Natalie drove to the pharmacy and filled his prescription, then took him to his house, carried his bag inside for him, fetched him a big glass of water, and admonished him to keep his phone by his bed and drink plenty of liquids.

As soon as she left, he took a pill, then eased his weight down on the bed. He unbuttoned his shirt, amazed that the simple task was so hard. He tried to lift a leg to toe off his shoe, but it hurt too much. Gingerly, he lay back on the pillows without trying to undress any further.

He closed his eyes, but all he could see behind his lids was Rachel gasping for air around Chief Hammond's choke hold.

He remembered diving for Hammond, praying that the chief would instinctively let go of Rachel and turn his weapon on him. It had been a desperate choice. Do nothing and let Rachel die. Or bet her life on Hammond's reaction.

He didn't find out whether she had survived until he'd woken up after surgery. A nurse had checked for him and reported that she had been released from the Emergency Room and her mother had picked her up.

He threw his arm over his face and pretended the dampness in his eyes was just a reaction to the pain. That was all. It wasn't because now he knew that he finally did believe in forever, but it was too little, too late.

He'd treated her so badly. He didn't deserve her love.

Chapter Eighteen

When Ash woke up, it was after six, and he was practically dying of thirst. He looked at the water glass Natalie had left on his nightstand. It was empty, damn it. He didn't even remember drinking it all.

He carefully sat up and closed his eyes against the dizziness he felt. After a few seconds, he slid his legs over the side of the bed and stood.

Without too much trouble, but with stars flashing in front of his eyes, he made it to the kitchen. So that was what Rachel was talking about when she said she saw stars.

Rachel. A profound sadness enveloped him. He wondered where she was. Still with her mom, probably. That's where she should be. Her mom would take care of her, support her, go with her to her doctor's appointments.

He couldn't blame her if she never wanted to see him again. After everything that had happened, maybe she'd thought better of including him in her life and the life of her baby—their baby.

As he stood staring into the refrigerator, the sadness morphed into a gaping emptiness that opened up inside him.

His parents' death had left a hole, of course. But over the years he'd filled that hole with anger, with determination, with ambition and, yes, with mindless, carefree fun.

This emptiness was different. It was hollow and bottomless. He was sure nothing would ever be able to fill it. He splayed his fingers on his chest, where the empty ache was centered, and felt his eyes sting.

"Get over it, Kendall," he snapped, doubling his hand into a fist and pounding his chest once. He was just feeling maudlin because he hurt and the pain pill he'd taken six hours before had worn off.

He grabbed a bottle of water, made his way to the couch, prepared to watch TV until he fell asleep. But all the files from his parents' murders were still stacked on the coffee table.

He set the bottle down and eased himself onto the couch, staring at the papers, reading a snatch of printing here and there.

—*in their beds on Christmas morning.*

—*tissue and blood under her fingernails.*

—*no suspects, no witnesses.*

Ash lay back against the armrest of the couch and closed his eyes. Campbell was dead, Hammond was apparently insane and the person who'd killed his parents was still out there, free.

And he was right where he'd always been. Alone.

RACHEL FINALLY MANAGED to convince her mother that she had to get back to work. Her mom, who had picked her up from the hospital after her examination, had held her captive for three days. She'd spent that time feeding her way too much and pulling out baby things she'd saved from Rachel's infancy. She'd been thrilled by Rachel's news about her pregnancy.

Any other time, Rachel would have enjoyed looking at the tiny little knit caps and matching coats, the little booties and all the cute pink tops and bottoms. But as thrilled as she was that her mother was happy about the baby, she was impatient to get back and see how Ash was doing. She'd called the hospital and found out he'd been discharged that morning, but when she tried his number, there was no answer.

So she'd put her foot down and insisted that her mother take her home.

"Or I'll call a cab," she threatened her. Sure enough that convinced her.

"A cab to your apartment will cost you two hundred dollars," her mother protested.

"At least," Rachel had said with glee.

Now she was back home, laden with quarts of her mother's famous chicken soup and a plastic container full of chocolate brownies.

She'd called Neil, who'd told her that Ash was at home recuperating. He'd also filled her in on the chief's arraignment and his plea.

"Did he say anything about breaking into my apartment?" she'd asked Neil.

"No. I asked him about that when I was interviewing him, but he acted like he didn't know anything about it."

"What do you think? Was it him?"

"I don't think so, but I can't be sure. I'm afraid the department shrink is right. She says he's had a psychotic break."

Rachel wondered how the chief's obsession with protecting his position and reputation had escalated to insanity and murder.

Now she looked at one container of soup and another of brownies and wondered why she wasn't already on her way over to Ash's house.

Of course, she didn't have to wonder. She knew. She was afraid to see him. She hadn't forgotten the sound of the door to his room closing. The way it had echoed in her mind like a prison door, locking her out of his life.

"I won't bother you," he'd said. But it hadn't been merely his words. It was also the look on his face. She'd never seen him look like that. His green eyes had been flat, almost gray. His face had been without expression and his voice had sounded dead. She'd known that was the end.

The sound of the door closing had been prophetic. It foretold the end of their relationship.

But he came to rescue you, her heart argued.

Right. Just like anyone in danger, her head responded.

She squeezed her temples between her palms, trying to stop the pointless argument. No amount of arguing or rationalization was going to change the truth.

She picked up her car keys where she'd tossed them on the kitchen counter and turned to put them in her purse. She looked at them more closely and realized she still had the key to Ash's house. Maybe she could slip the chicken soup and a few brownies into his refrigerator with a note.

Just a friendly note, she thought as tears stung her eyes. He'd rescued her. She could do something for him. It wouldn't mean anything.

When she got to Ash's house, she saw that his car was there and a light was on in the living room.

Was he awake? Maybe she should just leave the soup and brownies on his porch and call him after she got back home.

Coward. No. She'd knock and go in, give him the food and his key and thank him for saving her life.

She walked up the steps to the porch and knocked lightly. When no one answered, she used her key. Once inside, she saw Ash asleep on the couch. He was shirtless and she could see the bandage on his side. It was huge.

Her heart thudded. Just how bad had the gunshot been?

She'd called Neil when the hospital wouldn't tell her anything. He'd said it was practically a flesh wound. But she hadn't trusted his offhand answer.

She couldn't see much of Ash's face because he had an arm over his eyes. But his body looked thin and vulnerable. He'd always seemed so much larger than life to her. Like a superhero. But not now. Now he looked all too human. Human and breakable. Her throat clogged and her eyes filled with tears. How would she have lived if he'd died?

How was she going to live without him?

As she stood there, tears streaming down her cheeks, he stirred, sending her heart rate higher. She needed to set down the food and leave. She took a step and her keys rattled.

Ash lowered his arm. "Rach?" he whispered, opening his eyes to slits. "Damn it," he grunted.

Rachel didn't say anything. If she stood real still, maybe he'd think he was dreaming and go back to sleep.

"Is that the baby?" he asked, squinting up at her.

The baby? He *was* still asleep, dreaming.

"No, Ash, it's just some food. Go back to sleep."

"I hope she has your eyes," he whispered with a little smile as his eyes closed again. "Those weird, beautiful green-and-gold eyes."

Rachel's breath caught in a sob. She wanted to cover her mouth so Ash wouldn't hear, but her hands were full of soup, brownies and keys.

"Don't cry, Rach," Ash said. He held out a hand. "Come here."

She didn't know what to do except obey him. Carefully, she set the soup and the box of brownies on the end table and placed her keys beside them, then she stepped closer to Ash.

He caught her hand in his and grunted in pain. She

squeezed his hand. "Are you okay? Are you hurting? Where are your pain pills?"

He opened his eyes and looked at her. "I'm okay," he said. "How are you? How's the baby?"

She searched his face. "Are you still asleep?" she asked. "Because the baby's not born yet."

He laughed carefully. "I know that." His hand let go of hers and he touched her stomach. "Hey, baby," he said. "How're you doing?"

Tears streamed down Rachel's face. She couldn't tell if Ash was awake or drugged.

"My mom made you some chicken soup," she whispered through her tears. "And brownies."

"Mmm." His eyes closed again. "I like the things your mom makes. She made you."

Rachel brushed away the tears and took his hand again. "Ash, you need to wake up. I don't know what you took, but I don't like how you're acting."

He tugged on her hand and whispered something she didn't understand.

"What?" she asked, leaning closer.

He whispered again, but she still didn't catch it.

"Ash, I can't hear you."

He tugged on her hand again, so she leaned down close to his lips.

"What?" she whispered.

His other hand caught the back of her head and he kissed her. She gasped, surprised, and tried to pull away, but he wouldn't let her go.

"You want to know what I said?" he asked in a very low voice, his lips moving against hers.

She nodded, her breath catching at the feel of his mouth on hers, at his warm, soft breath drifting across her sensitive lips.

"I said when I opened my eyes, I thought you were a dream, my dream angel, come to watch over me. And I thought you were holding our baby."

Rachel's breath caught in a sob again.

"Don't cry," he murmured. "I'm sorry for all the times I've made you cry, and I don't blame you for not wanting anything to do with me, but—" He cradled her head and kissed her again. She kissed him back. It was a heartbreaking kiss. Everything she desired in the world was there in his kiss. If only he'd give it to her.

"Can I ask you something?" he whispered.

"Sure," she said. "Anything."

"Will you forgive me enough to let me be a part of our baby's life?"

Her heart soared. "Of course. I would never keep you from her."

"Her?" He lifted his head, wincing. "Her?"

"I don't know for sure, but it feels like a girl to me."

"Wow," he whispered, moving his lips erotically against hers again. "What about you?"

"What about me?" she asked, unsure of what he meant.

"Will you let me be a part of your life, too?"

Rachel blinked. "I—don't understand." She held her breath and waited to see what he said.

"Will you marry me?"

Rachel sat up straight. "What?"

"Ow. Careful!" he said, a pained smile on his face. "I'm a little sore."

"Oh, Ash, I'm sorry."

"It's okay," he muttered. He pushed himself carefully to a sitting position with a lot of grunts and groans.

Rachel felt helpless, watching him hurt so much just moving, but when she tried to help him, he only shook his head.

Once he was sitting up, she noticed that his face had drained of color. "Maybe you should lie down again," she said.

"Don't worry, I will in a minute. As soon as you answer me."

"An-answer you?"

"Rach, I want to marry you."

"No, you don't," she said hoarsely, pressing her hand to her throat. It felt like her heart was lodged there.

He brushed her lower lip with his thumb. "Yes, I do. More than anything I've ever wanted in my life."

She shook her head.

"Rach, I know what I want. Stop being so stubborn for once and just listen—" He stopped, gasping for breath. "Whew. I can't believe how weak I am."

"Ash, please lie down. If you pass out and fall off the couch—"

His eyes darkened. "I'm not going to pass out. I just need a straight answer. Will you marry me?"

She stared at him. "But you're Ashanova."

He grimaced. "I really hate that name. You know what name I like? Rachel Kendall."

Rachel's heart felt bruised. *Watch out,* she warned herself. *He's hurt and medicated. He can't be thinking straight.* But she couldn't resist saying the name out loud. "Rachel Kendall," she whispered.

"Mrs. Ashton Kendall," he said, smiling. But almost as quickly as his smile grew, it faded. He took her hand in his and placed it on his chest.

"Feel that?" he asked her.

"Your heart?"

"It's been empty for so long. I never trusted love. Never believed in forever. And I know I don't deserve you, but

I—" He stopped and cleared his throat. "I love you, Rachel. You have filled my empty heart."

His words filled hers, so full she was afraid it might burst. "I love you, too," she said, "more than you'll ever know."

"I know."

She leaned forward and kissed him again. Then she gingerly laid her head on his bare chest and closed her eyes, listening to his strong, steady heartbeat as he caressed her hair.

After a few moments she heard another sound. She giggled.

"Rach? What?" he asked drowsily.

"Your stomach's growling," she said, moving to stand up. "I'll warm you some soup," she said.

"Not yet. I want to hold our baby."

"Hold?"

Ash reached out and put his hand on her stomach. She smiled and laid her hand over his.

"Do you talk to her?" he asked.

Rachel nodded. "All the time."

"Is it okay if I do?"

"Of course," she said, her heart expanding with love for him.

His mouth widened in a heartbreaking smile. Then he looked down at her stomach. "Hi, baby," he said softly, his eyes glistening. "You don't know me yet but I'm your daddy."

* * * * *

REQUEST YOUR FREE BOOKS!
2 FREE NOVELS PLUS 2 FREE GIFTS!

Harlequin

INTRIGUE

BREATHTAKING ROMANTIC SUSPENSE

HI11B

*Harlequin Romantic Suspense presents the latest book
in the scorching new* KELLEY LEGACY *miniseries
from best-loved veteran series author Carla Cassidy*

*Scandal is the name of the game as the Kelley family fights
to preserve their legacy, their hearts…and their lives.*

Read on for an excerpt from the fourth title
RANCHER UNDER COVER

*Available October 2011
from Harlequin Romantic Suspense*

"**W**ould you like a drink?" Caitlin asked as she walked to the minibar in the corner of the room. She felt as if she needed to chug a beer or two for courage.

"No, thanks. I'm not much of a drinking man," he replied.

She raised an eyebrow and looked at him curiously as she poured herself a glass of wine. "A ranch hand who doesn't enjoy a drink? I think maybe that's a first."

He smiled easily. "There was a six-month period in my life when I drank too much. I pulled myself out of the bottom of a bottle a little over seven years ago and I've never looked back."

"That's admirable, to know you have a problem and then fix it."

Those broad shoulders of his moved up and down in an easy shrug. "I don't know how admirable it was, all I knew at the time was that I had a choice to make between living and dying and I decided living was definitely more appealing."

She wanted to ask him what had happened preceding that six-month period that had plunged him into the bottom of the bottle, but she didn't want to know too much about him. Personal information might produce a false sense of intimacy that she didn't need, didn't want in her life.

"Please, sit down," she said, and gestured him to the table. She had never felt so on edge, so awkward in her life.

"After you," he replied.

She was aware of his gaze intensely focused on her as she rounded the table and sat in the chair, and she wanted to tell him to stop looking at her as if she were a delectable dessert he intended to savor later.

Watch Caitlin and Rhett's sensual saga unfold amidst the shocking, ripped-from-the-headlines drama of the Kelley Legacy miniseries in

RANCHER UNDER COVER

Available October 2011 only from Harlequin Romantic Suspense, wherever books are sold.

Harlequin

SPECIAL EDITION

Life, Love and Family

Look for
NEW YORK TIMES AND *USA TODAY*
BESTSELLING AUTHOR

KATHLEEN EAGLE

in October!

Recently released and wounded war vet
Cal Cougar is determined to start his recovery—
inside and out. There's no better place than the
Double D Ranch to begin the journey.
Cal discovers firsthand how extraordinary the
ranch really is when he meets a struggling single
mom and her very special child.

ONE BRAVE COWBOY,
available September 27 wherever books are sold!